# Glutton for Pleasure

## Praise for Alisha Rai's *Glutton for Pleasure*

Rating: 5 Stars "Glutton for Pleasure is a sensual feast that will captivate the senses and leave the reader wanting more. Alisha Rai's writing is passionate and intense with an emotional undertone that will bring tears to the eyes and a smile to the lips. Glutton for Pleasure is the kind of erotic romance that can be enjoyed over and over again. Love, lust and satisfaction all combine to create a vivid story that can not be missed."

~ *ecataromance*

"Glutton for Pleasure by Alisha Rai is a decadently naughty read. Devi, Marcus, and Jace explore their newfound feelings for each other in a totally erotic and sensual way."

~ *Joyfully Reviewed*

"What was wonderful were the descriptions of Devi, told mostly through the eyes of Jace and Marcus, that were wholly in keeping with her ethnicity... Jace and Marcus' view of Devi was that she was this lush goddess, pillowy and full and perfect for them in her round, brown beauty. It was easy to understand their attraction for her and vice versa. The sex scenes were spicy and well done."

~ *Dear Author*

# Glutton for Pleasure

*Alisha Rai*

A Samhain Publishing, Ltd. publication.

Samhain Publishing, Ltd.
577 Mulberry Street, Suite 1520
Macon, GA 31201
www.samhainpublishing.com

Glutton for Pleasure

Print ISBN: 978-1-60504-335-7
Digital ISBN: 978-1-60504-470-5

Editing by Sasha Knight
Cover by Anne Cain



First Samhain Publishing, Ltd. electronic publication: March 2009
First Samhain Publishing, Ltd. print publication: January 2010

# Dedication

The Rom-Critters helped me take my writing to the next level, and I am so grateful. Special thanks to Liza O'Connor, Maggie Van Well, Nadia Williams, a.c. Mason, Lisa Troy, Ruby Ranidas, Wendy and Jean, excellent critters and even better authors.

# Chapter One

Thick, firm and curved just right, the shiny red skin stretched taut over hot seed and juice. Devi Malik squeezed the turgid flesh. *Perfect.*

The kitchen door burst open. “He’s back!”

“That’s nice.” Devi tossed the whole red chili pepper into the pan of sizzling shrimp and vegetables. She’d need to put in a larger order of the little buggers next week. When had spicy become the new black?

“You’re not even listening to me.”

Accustomed to her eldest sister’s dramatics, she took her time to stir the pepper evenly into the entrée before looking up. Rana stood in front of the commercial range, one fist propped on a curvy hip and a Cheshire-cat smile on her beautiful face. The Saturday dinner crowd would be piling in soon, and Devi needed to get in her groove, but long experience told her she wouldn’t get any peace until Rana vented whatever news she carried. “Sorry. What did you say?”

“He’s back. Mr. Tuesday Special.”

Devi’s hand jerked and hot oil splashed the inside of her wrist. “Damn it!” She dropped the spatula, yanked on the cold water at the faucet next to the stove and thrust her hand under the stream.

"Oh my God, are you okay?"

The icy water brought the painful throb down to a bearable sting. "Yeah, it's fine."

"You should be more careful. If I'd known the news would startle you that much, I would have warned you."

Devi cast a sharp glance at Rana's face. For just a second, she thought she caught a glimpse of shrewd cunning in her sister's eyes, but it vanished into simple concern. She withdrew her hand from under the water and dried it with studied casualness on the towel tucked into the front of her apron. "I'm sorry, I don't know what you're talking about."

With a flourish, Rana placed her orders on the board and lowered her voice to a whisper. Devi didn't know why she bothered. They were alone but for the two other chefs hard at work at the opposite end of the kitchen. "Jace is here."

Jace Callahan. Middle initial R. She knew that because she had gotten tired of Rana's silly nickname for the man and looked up his credit card receipt one night. Talk about stupid and pathetic.

In the face of her silence, Rana huffed an impatient breath. "Tall, dark and delicious? I know, I'm surprised too. He's not usually here on Saturdays."

Devi opened her mouth to deliver a blithe reply but the steam in front of her caught her attention. "Oh crap." She turned off the burner and fanned at the smoke. "Look what you made me do. You know the Jacobs send their plates back if everything isn't perfect."

Rana barely spared a glance at the pan. "It still looks fine to me."

"Shrimp isn't like other meat. It's not something you can overcook and have it still taste the same." *A distraction, please God.* Her mind raced. There was no way she could discuss her secret crush with either of her sisters—they could read her like a book.

She speared a shrimp, stuck it into her mouth and grimaced. Too chewy. She took too much pride in her craft to serve customers of The Palace chewy shrimp. Devi grabbed the pan and scraped the rest of the dish into a plate. She didn't believe in waste, so it would be her dinner later. The Jacobs would have to wait a little longer. Devi turned to the small dark woman at the far end of the room and raised her voice. "Asha, can you take the incoming? Redo table six. My sister," she continued, lowering her tone so only Rana would hear, "won't let me do my job. Don't you have customers to wait on?"

"All my tables are covered. Leena's gone for the night, and I need to get some paperwork done for her. And guess what? You're covering one of the tables for me."

No, no, no. Of course Rana hadn't brought up Jace for kicks and giggles. Devi's stomach sank under the suspicion of where her sister was going with this. "The Jacobs?" she stalled, and tried to look mildly curious. "You're right, they are so difficult, let me handle them."

Rana shook her head. "Jace said he wanted to meet his chef. So you need to serve him tonight."

In their small, family-owned restaurant, it wasn't unusual for the regulars to meet the chef. Hell, sometimes she even ended up waiting tables while she mingled if they were short on staff. How could she hand her secret object of lust his dinner, stand close enough to touch him and act as if he were just any other customer? She needed time to think about this, needed time to work this out. "Ummm..."

"Awesome, table eight."

Time up. "*Wait.*"

Rana turned with one hand on the door.

Damn it. "What's the order?"

Rana beamed. "Jace gave me the cutest little smile and asked if we could give him his usual even though it was Saturday. How could I say no?"

How, indeed. Though orders off menu always created a hassle for her, she couldn't blame her sister. If it had been her, she probably would have offered to feed him whatever he wanted by hand. Naked. Or by any other body part he preferred. Naked.

Rana sighed, as if reading her mind. "Aren't those black Irish types perfect? Brooding and charming, without even trying."

"I don't care how brooding he is. I'm just handing him his dinner."

Rana rolled her eyes. "Jeez, I'm kidding. Though it wouldn't kill you to flirt a bit. I swear, getting you a love life is a full-time job."

"I don't want to hear it." Lately Rana had been hinting, in her usual heavy-handed manner, that Devi needed to get out more. Ironic, really, since her overprotective big sisters had a well-known history of finding massive faults with the men she did finally bring home.

"Just be nice to him. I'm not telling you to strip naked. You save that for a date you're not cooking."

She wished.

"Oh, and by the way, he's got a guest. Double the order."

A guest? What? He always ate alone. Jealousy fired through her veins. After all, it was a Saturday night. He probably had a date.

*It could be his mother, his friend, anyone.*

*Or a date.*

Rana had already left and it wasn't like she could ask, anyway, without launching the Spanish Inquisition. She wiped her hands on her apron and pulled out onions. The specials were hers and hers alone, one for every day of the week, some of her favorite meals. When one was ordered, she did all of the prep and the cooking. The customers didn't know how small the kitchen was—they got a kick out of ordering something *prepared exclusively by the head chef*, as her middle sister and the restaurant's manager, Leena, had written on the menu.

Devi minced the garlic and ginger in a bowl of ice water to put aside while the onion turned transparent in the oil. Naturally, she had noticed when table eight had ordered her special twist on a thick lamb curry, her personal favorite, four weeks in a row. Noticing turned to curiosity when Rana had gushed over his attractiveness, tipping habits and overall perfection. One peep outside the little window turned her curiosity into full-blown lust. How could she have not snuck outside the kitchen to get a better look?

She added fresh tomato paste, yogurt and her secret spices to the onion and left it to simmer while she cut up chunks of lamb and dropped it in a separate pan.

Tall and broad-shouldered, he carried his arrogant good looks well—short dark hair, eyes the color of melted chocolate framed by thick lashes and a face that could have been chiseled by a master sculptor. He wore expensive suits, which wasn't unusual in and of itself, thanks to all of the office buildings surrounding their restaurant in downtown Lewiston. Unlike the rest of the after-work crowd, though, he didn't look at all tired or rumpled from the day's work or the Florida summer heat. Oh, and his butt always looked awesome. Devi made sure she caught at least one glimpse of the spectacular view during each visit.

His solitary status also set him apart and gave her foolish

heart another tug. Sure, people ate by themselves, but when he did it, he appeared incomplete. Not sad or lonely, but alone. All the same, he shrugged off any of the feminine attention he received, even Rana's teasing. Men made giant fools of themselves over Rana when she scowled at them—no one resisted her once she entered flirtatious mode. Jace seemed immune to her sister's charms though, focusing on his meal, and later, on the music and entertainment they provided.

Devi poured the curry and the ginger-garlic infusion over the now-golden lamb and tossed in diced potatoes. She left it to simmer while she plated two steaming bowls of white rice and pulled hot loaves of *naan* from the oven, automatically doubling their usual portion for two. After his first couple of visits, Devi had taken to sneaking a few extra pieces of the leavened bread into the cloth-covered basket. Jace always polished it off, using it until the end to soak up any remaining sauce on his plate. The chef within her appreciated his enjoyment of her food—he ate her favorite dish with a delicacy and tidiness at odds in such a big man.

As a woman, she loved the way his mouth looked closing over the bread.

She shivered, poured the curry into two earthenware bowls and added a garnish of cilantro to each. With a deep breath, she stood in front of the swinging doors, the large tray balanced on her hand.

*No big deal. You're not an agoraphobic, you've served people before. Hand him his meal, wish him a good dinner. Nice and professional. And maybe even mildly flirtatious.* She could use the practice, futile as it may be. She couldn't remember the last time she had batted her eyes at a man. No wait, she had never batted her eyes at a man. Maybe she should ask Rana for eyelash-batting lessons before she met Jace.

*No. Open the door, idiot. His dinner's going to get cold and then you'll have to deal with an irate, gorgeous man.* Before she could dream up any more procrastination, she shoved the door open with her hip and walked out. And then she stopped short, certain for a minute her vision had blurred by the steam in the kitchen. Two gorgeous Jaces sat at table eight, their faces presented in perfect profile. After a second look, she picked out subtle differences. Jace sat on the left, dressed in his requisite suit and indolently relaxed in his seat. The man on the right had the same dark, curling hair, but longer and shaggier, not shaped into a ruthless cut. Lines were etched around a slightly cruel mouth, and his gaze shifted constantly, his body tensed and coiled to spring at a moment's notice. His shoulders spanned an even wider width than Jace's, and the T-shirt and jeans he wore revealed a body as perfect as his brother's.

She had often thought it unfair she had been dropped into a family of gorgeous daughters, so she hoped this delicious pair of twins didn't have any siblings. No one could possibly compete with those two.

Jace smiled at something his doppelganger said and the identical man grinned back. Her breath caught at their masculine beauty.

*Well, that proves it. God has to be a woman.*

"Jace, are you listening?"

Marcus's identical twin gave him a guilty smile. The guy had been wired since he'd picked him up from the airport and dragged him out to eat at the small restaurant they were sitting in.

Marcus glanced around. All things considered, a nice place. They both liked spicy food, so Indian was a good choice. This one had a small, intimate air but seated a decent amount of people. The requisite gold and red silk furnishings were scattered about, of course, as were the elephant motifs, but the decorator had managed to do it in a way that suggested exotic rather than tacky. No incense, thank God. The stuff drove his allergies crazy. The small band of musicians on the corner stage strummed sitars and blew into flutes, creating a melodic counterpoint to the murmurs of the dinner crowd.

He caught sight of the pretty waitress across the room and wondered again if something had kindled in the month he'd been away on his business trip. Jace had been insistent they come here, and he and the woman had bantered with easy familiarity. She'd been cordial enough to Marcus, but with an underlying watchfulness, as if she was evaluating him on every level.

They both also liked spicy women, and in his experience, Indian was a good choice there too. Marcus studied her objectively. Golden skin, nice ass and shapely legs. She carried herself with the casual confidence of a model, her long blue black hair flowed in a silky straight fall and her tight black uniform showed off a killer body. She looked more complicated than easy. The women they usually screwed knew the score and agreed to it. A mind-blowing sexual experience, little conversation and silence later on. Easy, no love involved. Marcus rarely remembered their faces or names later.

He hadn't ridden a woman in months, and the tension and stress of the past few weeks of intense work had built the pressure in his system to the blowing point. He wanted nothing more than to pound his frustration into a willing woman.

Marcus tried to work up enthusiasm for their waitress, but barely managed a lukewarm stirring at the idea of her sandwiched between the two of them.

Oh well. Surely he'd be able to generate some excitement

once they were naked. Marcus took a drink of his beer. “She’s nice.”

“Huh?”

“Our waitress.”

“Yeah. Rana. But she’s not really your type.”

His shoulders tensed. Now that he thought about it, Jace had withdrawn lately. Marcus had deliberately ignored it while work distracted him, but he couldn’t put off facing it any longer. Was he unhappy with their casual lifestyle?

“Jace, what the hell is going on?”

The corner of Jace’s lip twitched, a sure sign he had something up his sleeve. “Okay. I brought you out here to meet someone.”

“No shit. Who?”

“Someone I think we’re both going to enjoy.”

Marcus relaxed. That was better. “You think?”

Jace shrugged. “I haven’t exactly met her myself.”

“Crap, Jace. You know we can’t just chase after anyone. We need someone who knows what we’re looking for here.”

“Don’t worry about it. I’ve spoken with her sister.”

“Yeah?” Marcus settled back in his seat and let his gaze drift over the restaurant. The other servers out front were male or older, but one of the bartenders, a young, buxom Latina, looked like she had potential. Bold, flirtatious eyes. She’d do for a night. “The bar looks good.”

“Later. Wait ’til you try the food.”

“Speaking of which, where is the food? You wouldn’t let me even grab a burger on the way. I haven’t eaten since this morning.”

“I didn’t want your appetite dulled.” Jace glanced around

before pausing. "Here she is." A surge of heat lit his eyes, warning Marcus even before he turned to the right.

At first he could only catch glimpses of the short woman behind the large tray of food, but as she came closer, the tray shifted out of the way.

*Soft.* She shared the same flawless golden skin and big dark eyes as the waitress. However, unlike their server's knowing and self-confident gaze, this one had a wary and vulnerable look about her that automatically turned the heat up, bringing out his protective and dominant instincts.

Her cheeks were round, flushed, from the heat of the kitchen no doubt, her lips full and pink. A ponytail restrained her long black curls at the nape of her neck. A spotless apron covered the sensible black jeans and snug T-shirt. She might be too plump to actually be called curvy, but Marcus approved of the slight roundness of her belly, the plush columns of her thighs. Her ass promised to be a luscious handful, and her breasts, outlined in her T-shirt, were large and pillowy. He couldn't imagine why he would want a hard, tight body below his when he could be plowing into the cushion of this one.

She hefted the tray in one hand and placed plates in front of both of them. Her breasts were at his eye level and he fantasized about leaning over and burying his face between them. Even the scent of the appetizing fare couldn't tear his gaze away.

"Smells great," Jace said.

Marcus knew when seduction was in his brother's low voice. Sure enough, Jace stared at her with as much vibrating intensity as Marcus felt. *Danger, danger.* This was not good. This was not good at all. Their father hadn't taught them much before leaving them in the hands of monsters, but not messing with good girls had definitely been hammered into them. This one's fresh and clean appearance practically screamed "good girl".

"Thanks." She placed the bowl of bread in the middle of the table and then held the tray clasped under her arm with a polite smile pasted on her face. "I'm your chef. I hope you enjoy your dinner tonight."

He loved her voice, low and a little bit throaty. It didn't match her wholesome image. He imagined her, sweet and innocent in a tiny white negligee and, please God, lace stockings, talking dirty in his ear with that sexy voice. His semi-hard cock lengthened and in a perfect inverse relationship, his conscience hushed. "What's your name?"

From the startled expression in her eyes, his request probably had come out as a growled order, but what could he do? He'd never experienced lust like this right off the bat, especially for a woman he would normally avoid like the plague. Cordial speech lay beyond his immediate capability.

"Devi Malik," Jace answered for her, his eyes locked on her face.

"That's right." She hesitated, her polite smile slipping a bit. "How do you know that?"

"I asked your sister." Jace turned to him. "Our waitress, Rana. Their other sister, Leena, manages. They own this place."

"Our mom actually owns the restaurant," she corrected.

"But you guys run it. I'm Jace Callahan and this is my brother Marcus."

A light of reluctant laughter lit her eyes. "Get out. I never would have guessed you were related."

Jace smiled. "Yeah, I guess it's stupid to introduce us that way, huh? It's a pleasure. I've been wanting to meet you."

"Why?"

Jace raised his left eyebrow, a move Marcus knew he had practiced in the mirror since they were ten. "Why, what?"

She laughed, the soft sound nervous. "Do you make it a habit to meet all of the employees at the places you eat?"

Jace's smile was slow and seductive. "Only the special ones."

"Oh."

"You have some excellent attractions here."

"Yes, our band is wonderful, aren't they?"

Jace hummed noncommittally.

"Is there anything else you need?" She stepped back from the table.

*You,* Marcus involuntarily thought. And then he realized, from the way both Devi and his brother stared at him, he hadn't just thought it.

"What?" Devi clutched her tray closer.

"You...must be a great cook," he finished lamely. Ah, hell. No one could ever say he was the suave one.

"Um, okay. Well, try the food first, and please let me know what you think."

"Wait." *Keep her here.* Marcus followed his instincts. "Sit with us."

"What?"

"Sit."

"What my brother means," Jace interrupted, with a warning glance at him, no doubt for his caveman behavior, "is that we would love to talk with you." He gave her a winning smile, flashing a set of dimples Marcus knew had won over more than one woman.

"Please." Marcus double-teamed her without mercy and

brushed the back of the hand clenched on the tray. Her skin was soft, the golden color warming through her flesh. The electrical current that passed through his fingertips surprised and dismayed him. *Trouble.* He slipped his hand under hers and drew it away from the tray to hold it. He swept his thumb over her small palm, marveling at how tiny it felt in his grip. Her nails were short and unpainted. Small calluses on her flesh were a testament to the work she did with her hands.

Her brow furrowed in bewilderment. "I—I can't do that."

"Why?"

"I'm working."

"Isn't part of owning a family business being able to set your own hours?" Jace asked practically.

"Yes...no. I don't..." She glanced back and forth between them, clearly overwhelmed.

Marcus stiffened. He didn't care what Jace had talked with the sister about. He'd bet money Devi hadn't known the score. She was too confused.

"Just so you know, I already asked your sister's permission. No one's going to fire you for eating your dinner with us," Jace teased.

At the mention of her sister, her eyes filled with obvious hurt before anger took its place. "Ah. I get it. Did my sister put you up to this?"

Marcus glanced at Jace, but he shrugged. "Up to what?"

She smiled, but it seemed forced. "You can drop the act. And while she might have pitched it to you as a way to get me out of my shell, I can assure you that this is more an insult than a kindness." Devi withdrew her hand. "Two of you were overkill. Enjoy your dinner." She pivoted and stalked toward a shadowy corridor off the main dining room. Marcus couldn't help but watch all of the glorious jiggling that accompanied her furious exit.

Jace cocked his head. "That went well."

The back office door slammed against the wall with a satisfying thunk.

Rana jumped and straightened from where she shuffled some papers on the office desk. Whatever she glimpsed in Devi's expression made her eyes widen in what looked like fear.

Good. She better be afraid. "Where's Leena?"

Rana licked her lips. "I told you, she had to go somewhere tonight. Why?"

Devi stepped inside and kicked the door closed with her foot before starting toward her sister. "I don't want any witnesses when I kill you."

"*Wait.*" Rana darted behind the big chair and swiveled it so it stood between them. "Are you mad?"

"Hell yes, I'm mad. Do you have any idea how embarrassing that was? How dare you tell them—our customers, a regular customer—to flirt with me like that? What did you say? That your poor desperate sister hadn't had a date in a year and needed to get her ego stroked a little? That I needed some practice?"

"What?"

Devi stopped a few feet away from the chair. "I'll tell you what I told them—you shouldn't have had them both go for it."

Rana stilled. "They both were into you?"

"Yeah, they followed your instructions to the letter. Good job."

"Hey, wait just a second. If they were checking you out, I had nothing to do with it. I admit, I knew Jace liked you. He's been pestering me for weeks to tell him your name. Quite frankly, it wasn't 'til last week I agreed. I wanted to make sure he had his shit together." Rana's shoulders tensed imperceptibly. "You said the brother was hitting on you too?"

"Like you don't know." She didn't believe a word Rana said. Beneath the anger lay a bone-deep hurt and a wicked sense of loss. Anyone else, she would have written off, but this had been her secret fantasy man. She knew she didn't have a chance, but no woman wanted to look desperate in front of a man she dreamt of late at night while tucked away in bed with a romance novel. To think of Rana patiently explaining her poor, dear sister's plight while Jace and his brother listened in sympathy—she just wanted to crawl under a rock somewhere.

"Devi." Rana's tone brooked no-nonsense. "Okay, so here's the deal..." She trailed off.

"Look, sis, I need to go cook. I don't have time for this."

"They share women, okay?"

Devi's jaw dropped. Literally, she felt it unhinge. "What?"

Rana's lips compressed into a thin line. "I should have warned you before I sent you out there, but I had no idea if it was true, or if you would just hit it off with Jace by himself. There's a lot of rumors—too many for them to be discounted. Jace is a pretty high-profile attorney so they're well-known here even though his brother travels a lot. You don't hear these things 'cause you're always hiding away, but I do. They're, like, the kings of one-night stands. And they do it together. Always. I don't think I know a single woman who's fucked just one of them."

Devi shook her head. "How?"

"Huh. Okay. You know how you're fucking one guy, so the other one, he—"

"Jesus, Rana, I don't want a blow-by-blow. I know how

these things work." Now she felt as uncomfortable as Rana looked. "I read enough." Well. Wow.

"Why would you think that I set them up? I know the brother is new, but Jace has been salivating over you for a month. I can't believe you didn't see it. Shit, I thought that was the reason you kept sneaking out of the kitchen, so you could make junior high googly eyes at each other. I just wanted to give you a push, an excuse to talk to him."

"Stop teasing."

"I'm not teasing."

"Right."

"He's been watching you, Dev. Every time you looked away, his eyes were glued on you. He eats you up." A perplexed frown creased Rana's smooth brow. "Why don't you believe me?"

"Because if you and I were in the same room, no one would be looking at me."

She immediately regretted her words, but they had slipped out before she could stop them. Rana inhaled sharply, and then glared. Devi suppressed a sigh. Even outraged, Rana looked good. "I can't *believe* you just said that. Like you're a hag."

Not a hag. Just a normal woman. In her experience, super-attractive types always went for super-attractive types. "We all know who the pretty one is."

Rana opened her mouth and closed it again. To Devi's surprise, her eyes shimmered. "Oh, Devi. I'm so sorry," she whispered, and pressed her fingers to her lips.

Her soft heart folded right into itself. She sighed and walked over to draw her sister into her arms. Since Rana reached almost six feet in her heels, and Devi wore her usual discreet wedges, the one-foot difference pushed her face right into Rana's boobs. Accustomed to the odd position, she turned her face to speak. "Hey, you have your period, or something? You're so emotional," she attempted to tease. "I didn't mean that the way it sounded. I promise, I don't hate you for being beautiful."

Rana gave a choked laugh and disentangled their arms. "I'm only going to say this once. I've been flirting with that man since he started coming here. I figured he was gay until I saw the way he tracked you. I can't believe you think I set them up to hit on you. You've seen them. I doubt there's anyone in the world who could make those two do anything they don't want to."

Devi pondered that. Truly, she didn't see either of them faking anything. Especially Marcus, he seemed so raw and real. "So let me get this straight. You wanted me to go out there and see what would happen with two men? Who are you and what have you done with my sister? You know, the one who went out and bought a fake handgun to terrify my prom date?"

Rana drew herself up to her full height. "I've decided that Leena and I haven't done you too many favors by keeping you so sheltered. You're missing out on life and it's partly our fault."

"I like my life."

"But, Devi, all you do is work, work, work and go home. It's like you don't care anymore, and you're not even twenty-seven. You should be living it up and enjoying yourself, and you're stuck in a rut. You haven't so much as looked at a man since Tarek—"

"I don't want to talk about him," she said, her voice hard. A year mended battered pride, but she didn't want to discuss a relationship that ended in such mortification.

Sadness and regret flashed through Rana's dark eyes. "Okay. All I'm saying is, you need to go have some fun, shake yourself up. And you need to remind yourself what a beautiful, gorgeous woman you are, especially if you really believe that nonsense you just spouted. There is nothing wrong with having a fling, a one-night stand, as long as you know the score. If these guys float your boat—and why wouldn't they?—go float theirs. Just remember everything I've told you. And go into it prepared so you don't get hurt." She dropped her hand and stepped back. "And with that, I am officially out of the equation, grasshopper. Do me proud." Rana walked to the door and opened it.

"Hey." Devi didn't continue speaking until Rana looked over her shoulder. "Can you get Asha to cover the kitchen for the rest of the night?"

Her eyes widened in surprise before a slow smile spread over Rana's face. "Abso-fucking-lutely, darling."

# Chapter Two

The silent office pulsed with hidden possibilities in the wake of Rana's absence.

A ménage, huh? She had told Rana the truth—more than a few ménage stories were stored on her hard drive. Though her real-life sexual experience may have been limited to a couple of discreet affairs, she found the idea of two men intriguing. To say the least.

She imagined herself sandwiched between the two identical men, multiple hot hands running over her nude flesh. Would their bodies look the exact same? Would she be able to feel a difference in their hands?

In their cocks?

A shudder ran through her and she paced to the small mirror hanging on the wall. The woman staring back at her did not entertain thoughts like these. That woman loved puppies and children and whiled her days away fulfilling familial obligation and living up to expectations. That woman waited patiently for a man to come along and make the first move. That woman would be happy with a sex life that was limited to a once-a-week missionary-style fuck.

Rana certainly had her number. Had her sister so much as whispered a breath of gossip regarding the Callahans before Devi met them, she would have either been too nervous or too self-conscious to so much as stammer out a hello.

Nobody could call Rana an idiot, either. She knew masculine interest the way Devi could differentiate between kinds of rice. Deep in her heart, after speaking with the twins face-to-face, Devi knew Rana was right. Unless Jace acted like this with every woman, and she had observed him enough to be fairly certain he didn't, he was indeed attracted to her.

As for the brother, whew. His chocolate eyes had practically singed a hole through her. While Jace might quietly maneuver to get his own way, she had the feeling Marcus plowed through life, taking what he wanted with little regret.

She hadn't slept with a man in almost a year now, not since her doomed relationship with Tarek had disintegrated. Not because she had been traumatized, but out of disillusionment. She couldn't call any of her past sexual experiences particularly spectacular. When she considered all of the boyfriends she'd ever been with, none of them had made her heart race or her palms sweat. She'd given herself better orgasms reading erotica than from having sex. After those orgasms, she lay awake in her bed, her super-sensitive flesh rubbing against the high-thread-count cotton, and wondered if she could experience even a tenth of that fictional passion. How many nights had she wished for a man who could rouse her to the height of lust and quench the desire inside her? A man who could respond to some of the darker desires she kept hidden?

Now she had two men—if she hadn't scared them off completely—who could fill that need. A mind-blowing sexual experience, a fantasy fulfilled. By their own pattern of behavior, she would never even need to see them again. So the question became, what was she going to do about it?

Devi stared at her reflection, and out of habit, catalogued all of her flaws in a single sweep. She and her sisters had inherited their father's eyes, but physically, the three of them shared nothing else. Rana was the undisputed beauty of the family, and athletic Leena wasn't too far behind. Devi considered it a sign of progress that she could look at Rana's curvy body and perfectly formed face today and feel only a slight twinge of envy. There had been a time during the worst of her chubby, pimply and frizzy adolescence when the sight of Ravishing Rana would send her into a deep depression.

The chubbiness had never left, unfortunately, and the frizziness returned when it rained. Hey, at least her skin had cleared. *Yay.*

No frizz tonight though. She slipped the cloth-covered elastic from her ponytail. Men had found her hair sexy in the past. She could make the most of it. The black riotous mane of ringlets fell to her shoulders. She ran her hand through the hair, purposely tousling the strands before studying her clothes with a critical eye.

She removed the apron and hung it on the hook next to the mirror before she grabbed the hem of her T-shirt and pulled it over her head. Underneath she wore a tight black tank top. The built-in shelf bra waged a mighty battle to keep her heavy chest contained and lifted. She only wore the tank under shirts when all of her bras were in the laundry—the deep cleavage it created made her too self-conscious to wear on its own.

She straightened in front of the mirror and sucked her belly in. She even managed to keep up the flat plane for about thirty seconds, but then she had to exhale. Devi frowned at the pooch. *Ahh, well. Too late to start doing crunches. Tomorrow,* she promised herself. Tomorrow she would do fifty right after getting up. Or maybe she would start the day after that. No one should ever exercise on a Sunday.

The small walnut desk yielded Leena's small bag of

cosmetics and a compact. Though she rarely used the stuff herself, she knew a few tricks. She applied black kohl and smoky eye shadow with quick strokes, until her eyes looked deep and mysterious. The lipstick was a bit redder than she preferred, but the dramatic look worked well for tonight.

Recapping the tube, she peered back into the mirror. Oh yes. This woman she could be tonight. Two men? Please. This woman could take three or more with little worry.

This woman wouldn't let silly things like expectations and social constraints get in the way of one amazing night of pleasure.

And it would just be for one night, as Rana had said. She wouldn't kid herself. Ménages were about the sex—relationships couldn't come out of them. She grimaced to think of the awkwardness of that. She couldn't imagine dating one brother while both of them knew she had slept with the other. No, one night of pleasure.

But what a night.

Devi tousled her hair a bit more and nodded definitively before leaving the office. Her confidence and resolution diminished a bit with every step, until she hovered at the mouth of the hallway. The sounds of light laughter and the tinkling of silverware came from the main dining room.

What would she say? Could she really just sit there in her family restaurant and vamp them? Being a nonconformist was all well and good, but at the end of the day, the staff worked for her family. What would they think of her?

What if the brothers had already left? What if—?

"Excuse me."

The deep rumble from behind her pulsed a shot of adrenaline through her veins. She whirled around so fast she overbalanced on her heels. Strong hands grasped her around the waist and saved her from landing straight on her butt.

She looked up. And up. And up. Into a pair of sinfully beautiful brown eyes, framed by a thick layer of lashes.

"Oh. Hi. Marcus, right?"

"Good memory."

"What are you doing here?"

Marcus cocked his head. "Men's room."

Of course. He wouldn't just be lurking in the hall waiting for her.

"What are you doing here?"

She brought her attention back to his unwavering gaze. "Um, office."

"Ah. And here I thought you might be waiting for me."

Warmth wormed under her skin at the low huskiness in his voice. She licked her lips, some of her daring returning under his flirtation. "Maybe I am."

A black eyebrow arched and he glanced down. "You changed. I like this shirt better."

"I was getting hot. That's all." The longer he stared at the massive amount of chest she flaunted, the hotter she got.

His lips curled in a slow smile, a dimple playing peekaboo in his cheek. "Me too."

"You—you don't need to keep holding me up, you know. No danger of falling now," she joked in nervousness.

They both looked down at his hands where they clasped her hips. Instead of withdrawing, he tightened his grasp and sent tingles racing over her flesh by sweeping his thumbs down until they rested on her pubic bone. On the upsweep, his thumb crept under her tank top and raised it so a small strip of flesh became visible. The heat of his thumb on her bare stomach burned where he rubbed back and forth in a gentle caress.

"I want to keep holding you."

Well, clearly.

"You changed something else too. Your hair, your makeup."

Gads, how embarrassing for him to know she had primped and polished for him and his brother.

"I like your hair down." Marcus withdrew one hand to twine a ringlet around his finger. He stretched the curl down until it straightened, and then let go. He used the hand on her hip to draw her closer, before tracing her upper lip with his forefinger. "But you should be careful with that lipstick, sweetheart. Naked, your lips are gorgeous, but when you paint them that color, you're just inviting a man to think all sorts of nasty things."

His finger rested on her lower lip, not exerting any pressure, just tantalizing her with the promise. Their gazes locked, and without thinking, she opened her mouth. He inhaled sharply as she drew him inside, savoring the clean taste of his finger in her mouth.

Delicious.

As if a switch had been tripped somewhere inside of her, wildfire raced through her veins. She wanted to rip off his clothes and find out how every inch of his body tasted. She applied a slight suction, once, twice, drawing him in deeper before she backed off, his finger emerging from her mouth with a small wet sound.

A ruddy flush colored high on his cheekbones, and his breathing had sped up. "Holy Christ. You're amazing." He grasped both hips again and pulled her tight against him, until she could feel the tantalizing promise of his erection throbbing against her belly.

"This isn't fair. You started without me."

Devi jerked in surprise, but Marcus controlled her by expediently wrapping an arm around her. He looked behind her. "Your loss."

Devi didn't dare turn around in case she completely lost her nerve, but she could feel the warmth of Jace's body as his footsteps came to rest right behind her.

"So you decided we weren't faking our interest, huh?"

She tensed and glanced at him over her shoulder. A gentle light shone in his eyes, his smile teasing, and she immediately felt a little more at ease. "I'm so sorry about that outburst. If you had any idea how meddling my family can be—and I didn't think you could possibly both be attracted to me—but then my sister told me..."

"What?" Jace prompted when she trailed off.

"That you like to, you know. Share women," she finished in a mumbled rush.

Jace gave a low chuckle. "Oh, baby. You have no idea at all what we like." He lowered his head until his lips hovered just above hers. "Do you want to find out?"

She felt like a rabbit surrounded by two large predators. Except she didn't mind being prey.

An imperceptible nod and Jace gave a large sigh. "Thank God." As if her nod broke his restraint, he slipped a hand under her hair to cradle her neck and tipped her head.

He didn't bother with a gentle, exploratory foray. No one had ever kissed Devi like that, like they were dying for her taste. Jace's tongue swept inside without asking permission, and his hand held her head still while he plundered within.

She heard a sudden groan and then hot hands covered her breasts. She moaned into Jace's mouth as Marcus expertly cupped them, his fingers pinching the sensitive tips hard.

*This should feel uncomfortable,* Devi marveled. *Turning your head and kissing one man while another fondled you from the front?* At the very least, there should have been some awkwardness, right?

The rush of cool air on her stomach startled her out of the pleasure of exploring Jace's mouth. She realized Marcus had taken advantage of her compliance to drag up her tank top. She whimpered as the cotton rasped her nipples, the air drifting over the heated tips, until they were bare...

In the hallway of her family's restaurant.

Her eyes popped open and she jerked away. Unfortunately, with Marcus in front of her, and Jace behind, the only way she could go was to the left. Smack into the wall.

"Ow!"

"Are you okay?"

"What's wrong?"

Their words tumbled over each other as four hands pulled her away from the wall. "I'm fine," she mumbled, and tugged at the neckline of her top until all her important parts were tucked away. "I-I can't do this."

Marcus stiffened, his face blanking, while Jace frowned and then nodded. "I'm sorry, you seemed like you were into it."

"I am," she reassured them in a rush. God forbid they get the wrong idea. "Here. I meant I can't do this here. Anyone could see."

Two pairs of broad shoulders relaxed, and Jace smiled. "Ever been watched?"

A shudder ran through her and her nipples hardened even more. She had never gone for such a kinky proposition before, but suddenly the idea of someone watching her, being aroused by her, while she in turn gave in to passion, really rocked her boat.

No, not yet. Right now the only people she wanted watching her body were these two.

Devi cleared her throat. "I have no intention of having sex here."

"But somewhere, right?"

Devi smiled at the bite of impatience in Marcus's voice. "Yeah."

"Our place?"

She hesitated. No, she didn't want to give up complete control. "I'd rather go to my apartment, if that's okay?"

"If you said you wanted to head to the dumpster in the alley, we wouldn't be far behind, sweetheart," Jace said.

Marcus snorted. "And that's saying something, if you knew how fastidious he is."

"Okay. Um, let me go get my purse." She inched around Marcus and walked to the office door on watery legs. She heard them approaching and turned swiftly to meet them. "I need a minute, please. I'll be right out."

Without waiting for a response she slipped inside the door and closed it behind her. She collapsed against it and heaved a deep breath. She looked across the room to the mirror, taking in the swollen lips and rumpled clothes reflected there.

A slow smile curled the lips of the vixen in the mirror.

Oh, yes, indeed. She could definitely handle this.

# Chapter Three

Jace wanted to rub his hands with glee and howl at the moon.

Although that would hardly be mature.

He glanced down at the voluptuous little siren walking silently in front of them as they left through the back door of the restaurant. Luck fell on their side, and they encountered no one on the way. It wouldn't take a genius to pick up the vibes of sex and intent around the three of them.

Not that he or Marcus would care, but Jace had the feeling Devi might have expired on the spot had a staff member or customer so much as glanced in their direction. Her veneer of courage and bravado was paper thin, her excitement and rampant sexual curiosity just barely outweighing her reserve. Jace didn't want anything to tip the scales in the wrong direction.

He'd been working toward this for weeks, since he'd first seen Devi and felt a visceral physical reaction in his gut, a primal need to stake his claim. He'd pestered Rana with questions and bombarded her with requests until the woman had agreed to introduce them. Not before threatening to cut his balls off if he hurt her baby sister, of course. He had no intention of hurting anyone, though. He had a happy ending in mind.

One for him, his brother and the woman blossoming under their undivided attention.

He couldn't pinpoint the exact moment he had become tired of the casual threesomes in which he and Marcus had engaged for over a decade now. When he had seen the quiet little chef slip out of the kitchen, he'd taken a body blow. He was a normal, healthy thirty-five-year-old man who liked sex, loved women, but he'd never before had such an immediate reaction to a woman. Though he felt vaguely stalker-ish, he had watched her whenever he could catch a glimpse and chatted up the staff at the restaurant. Except for the bartender, who found Devi a bit too reserved and a little snooty—and by that time, Jace had become so infatuated he wanted to punch the guy for daring to malign her—they spoke of her with affection and respect.

Her sidelong glances had given him hope she noticed him as well. The idea pleased him to no end. Love at first sight—a couple of months ago, he would have scoffed at such a ridiculous idea. Now, well...perhaps they didn't know each other well enough to call it love, but he would reserve judgment.

He hadn't wanted to make a move, though, until his brother came back into town. Jace wanted a woman who could love both of them wholeheartedly. Marcus was his other half—he couldn't imagine having a relationship with a woman on his own. If Devi could be that woman...Lord, that would be perfect.

Of course, he would bring up his intentions later, once they had Devi snared and Marcus was too far gone on her to come up with any stupid objections.

Just call him Mr. Ulterior Motive.

They followed her into the small alleyway behind the restaurant. The balmy Florida air lifted the strands of her dark hair. Scents of rich, savory food drifted from the building. Since he associated the smell with Devi, it made him harder.

She turned to face them and licked her lips, the only sign of her nervousness. “I live one block over, so I rarely drive.”

“Jace has a nice car. This is a good neighborhood, but I hate to leave it out all night. We can all just ride over there together.”

Her dark eyes widened, no doubt in response to Marcus’s all-night comment, but she nodded.

When they turned around the corner of the restaurant into the front parking lot, Jace stopped. “If you want, we can just get the car and you can stay here in the shadows. So no one will see us leaving together.”

She considered it, but then her rounded little chin firmed and she shook her head resolutely. “No, it’s okay. I don’t care who sees us.”

Jace knew she was lying, but he felt proud of her in any case. Marcus expressed his silent approval by stroking a hand over the curve of her ass, and she jumped just a bit.

His car served as a slight distraction for Devi. She let out a low whistle and shot them both an incredulous look. “This isn’t a nice car. This is a thing of beauty.” She ran a small hand over the hood of the silver Jaguar sports sedan in a worshipful manner.

Jace felt a corresponding lick of fire up his spine. He couldn’t resist a woman who could respect a car.

He tossed the keys to Marcus and ignored his brother’s knowing chuckle. Grabbing Devi’s hand, he opened the back door and just managed to keep from stuffing her inside. He slipped in next to her.

“Where do you live?”

As she rattled off her address, Jace watched her fingers

caress the butter-soft leather of the seat with unknowing sensuality. He counted three strokes before he groaned and gave in, reaching for her. "Drive." He bit the command out, and then slid over and pressed her against the door, his lips falling on hers, his hands tight around her waist.

He tried to gentle his touch, but the sweet taste of her mouth made him as crazy as it had back at the restaurant. Her body turned toward him, rounded arms slipped around his neck. Her lips immediately parted for the forceful thrust of his tongue, and the soft submission inherent in the gesture made him even hotter. He plundered until they were both gasping for breath, barely hearing the purr of the motor as Marcus drove.

Jace swept a hand up her body until the weight of a heavy breast filled his palm. He had fantasized more times than he could count about her amazing breasts, imagined her straddling his chair and feeding him topless. He drew back a bit as he pulled the stretchy neck of her abused tank top down until a delectable breast spilled out, propped on the shelf of the tight shirt. He mourned the lack of illumination, but the passing lights of other cars at least gave him glimpses of the plush golden flesh and upthrust little brown nipples.

Unable to resist, he cupped her and bent down to draw upon the exposed nipple. At the touch of his lips her body bowed against him. Her hands tangled in his hair to hold his head tight against her. A small moan emerged from her mouth.

Marcus groaned in response from the driver's seat, and Jace knew without looking that half his brother's attention was on the rearview mirror. "You like that, don't you, baby?"

When she didn't respond, Jace rasped her nipple with his teeth and gently grasped her wrists, pulling them from his hair to pin them against the seat. The way she strained against the small restraint, the excitement he could see shimmering in her eyes, just about undid him. "Answer him."

Devi shook her head, bewilderment and passion turning her eyes black. "What?"

"You like me kissing you? Sucking on your sweet breasts?"

She nodded mutely. He leaned down and lapped at the tip. "Say it."

She shuddered and stared at him as if she had never seen him before. The slight forcefulness in his tone during sex always surprised women at first—out of the bedroom, he might be a little less rough around the edges than his brother, but both of them had fairly dominant tendencies.

"I love it. Please—don't stop." She arched her chest toward his mouth, and he obliged, keeping her hands where they were. He wanted her to be accustomed to the feeling of sensual helplessness.

Her moans rose with every tug of his mouth and she undulated beneath him. The sweet spicy scent of her skin and her arousal made his head spin.

His normally alert senses ignored the halt of the car and the cutting of the engine. He only came up for air when the door behind Devi's back abruptly opened and she spilled into Marcus's waiting arms.

"Which apartment?" Marcus growled and set her on her feet while Jace climbed out and slammed the door.

"104," she gasped, and tried to jerk up her shirt.

Jace could have told her it was a wasted move, but before he could utter a word, Marcus scowled and pulled her hand away. "Don't cover yourself."

Her body quivered with vibrating tension. "But *anyone* could see."

Unlikely, Jace thought. She lived at the end of the very

quiet street, and the other four apartments in the small bungalow-style building were dark and deserted. Plus, their bodies blocked hers from easy view.

Why should he reassure her? If he read her right and she really was the perfect mate for them, the forbidden aspect of it would only ratchet her hunger up.

Marcus must have concurred, because he reached out and tugged hard against the opposite strap of her shirt. The cotton gave way quickly, and he pulled the other cup down to bare her entire chest. "I don't care."

"Well, I do." She glared at them and moved to cover her flesh.

Marcus growled and loomed over her. "Don't hide them. I want your tits bare. They're gorgeous."

"Maybe I don't care what you want."

"In bed, you obey me, Devi."

She snorted. "Like hell. I agreed to have a little fun. I didn't sign on for some crazy submissive role."

The light of battle flashed in Marcus's eyes. "Baby, don't you get it? This is the way we play. We want your tits stripped, they're stripped. If you don't want to play the game, tell us now before we go too far. You aren't comfortable with this, say no, and we leave. Otherwise—this is us."

She looked at Jace and he tried to convey reassurance through the layers of lust clouding his brain. Truth be told, he was feeling just as raw as Marcus. He knew they were asking a lot of her, but Marcus was telling the truth, trying to give her fair warning—they wouldn't be able to hold back anything once they were in the sack. Better for her to be aware of all their kinks before she found herself completely at their mercy. Once again, her little chin stuck up. "I want a safe word."

Jace chuckled, amusement piercing his haze of need. “We aren’t going to be flogging you, honey.” With a wink, he added, “We left our whips in the other car. But if it makes you feel better, use ‘red’ if you want us to stop.”

“Red is good. Red I can remember.”

“So you going to play with us, baby?”

Devi hesitated and then gave a small smile. “I guess it can’t hurt, just for one night.”

One night? The hell with that. But they had plenty of time to sort that out.

Her hands fluttered over her exposed chest and Marcus grasped one. “Then you need to obey. You cover those luscious little nipples again, and you’re going to get punished.”

She swallowed, licked her lips.

With deliberate intent, she lifted her free hand and crossed her arm over her chest.

Jace inhaled. A muscle jumped in Marcus’s cheek, but otherwise his face was still, eyes blazing. “Oh, baby. Your ass is mine.” He turned and strode toward the first-floor apartment, Devi in tow and Jace following behind her.

“Wait.”

“Keys,” Marcus snapped, all the more menacing for his calm.

She fumbled with her purse, and Jace groaned at the subsequent jiggling of her breasts. Finally, she located a large key ring and hesitated. “I hope you guys are going to make some allowances for a newbie.”

Jace leaned in close and nipped her small earlobe. “Don’t worry so much, sweetheart. Just go with the flow.” He took the keys and dropped them into Marcus’s outstretched palm.

The lock clicked open, an ominously loud sound,

accompanied by their heavy breathing and the rustle of the palm trees. The door squeaked open and Marcus pulled her into the darkness of her apartment.

Devi's world spun as she was swept into her foyer, Marcus's hand wrapped around her wrist, Jace's around her waist. Moonlight streamed through the windows of the adjoining living room, but the relative darkness rendered her belongings into something altogether unfamiliar, a suitable backdrop for her mood.

*Just go with the flow.* She'd never done that before. All her life, she had played by the rules and stayed safe. Devi could finally appreciate the allure of being a little bad, of venturing outside of her comfort zone. The unease of the unknown mixed with excitement and anticipation, until her brain swam with the heady brew. All of her senses felt as if they had been sharpened. The cool air swept over her bare breasts, underscoring her vulnerability, while the lust simmering off her soon-to-be lovers made her high with feminine power.

Nonetheless, a shot of awkwardness bloomed when the door shut behind Jace with a thud. She turned to him and cleared her throat. "Do you want something to drink?"

Marcus's dark chuckle warned her. "You."

Before she could respond, calloused hands spun her around until her back met the wall. Her hip bumped the small foyer table, and she dimly heard the thud as knickknacks fell to the carpeted floor.

Marcus captured her lips in a bruising kiss that asked no permission—not that she would have denied him. Her nipples rubbed against the cotton of his T-shirt, the cool fabric tightening them further. She grabbed the hem of his shirt, and he took the hint, bunching it up in both hands, breaking their kiss only to pull it over his head and toss it to the side. Her hands fell to the wide leather belt around his waist, fumbling to release the catch.

She had only pulled the buckle free when her jeans loosened. Marcus's clever hands pushed the denim over her hips and took her panties with them. *Thank God he won't see them.* Plain white cotton bikinis did not scream seductive risk-taker. Had she known she would be in this position, she would have dug out some black lace. Well, she didn't own any black lace, but she could have made a quick run to a lingerie store.

*As if you could have predicted this.* Standing naked but for a small cotton tank top twisted around her waist in front of two gorgeous men. Only in her wildest fantasies.

Marcus stepped back, his fingers going to the buttons of his jeans. His chest rose and fell with his heavy breaths, and his broad shoulders looked even larger outlined in shadows.

The sound of a zipper turned Devi's head to the left just as Jace kicked free of his pants. She wished she could turn on the overhead light, the better to see their hard bodies, but feared it would break the spell and expose all of her own flaws. The sliver of moonlight played peekaboo on his flesh, providing a glimpse of a hard six-pack, straining biceps and the outline of an impressive cock when he turned in profile for a too-brief moment.

Marcus crowded her against the wall again, his leg insinuating between her own. The rough hairs rasped against her soft inner thighs, and his erection felt as long and promising as Jace's had looked. She gasped as he pushed a hand into her hair and tilted her head to the side. His lips fastened to the sensitive flesh of her neck hard enough to leave a mark in the morning.

Not that she would mind. Her eyes almost rolled back in

her head as he kept her steady for his pleasure, his other hand sweeping down her body to cup the curve of her buttock. She twined her arms around his neck, her fingers tunneling into his hair, and tried to find purchase for the dizzying pleasure. His large hand spread over her cheek and squeezed in concert with the sucking of his mouth.

She bit her lip to keep back the cry as he clenched her ass and lifted her into the cradle of his hips, his hard cock finding a perfect home in the wetness dripping down her thighs.

He pulled back. "Don't hide what you're feeling. I want to hear every noise you make." His voice was harsh, the flash of white teeth in the darkness making her even wetter. "Otherwise, how will I know if you like...this?"

He used two fingers to open the lips of her vagina before penetrating her with just the tip of his cock. She moaned in combined relief and distress and tightened her fingers in his hair. She lifted one leg to wrap around his waist and strained to get even closer, to climb inside him if possible.

He seemed agreeable enough. He used both hands under her bottom to hoist her up until he held her suspended against the wall by the strength of his arms, just the first inch of his cock teasing her with the promise of its power. "Wrap both legs around me." When she complied in an instant, he rewarded her with a quick, hard kiss. "Good girl."

The first thrust of his hips gave her just a hint of his size; his second, more forceful thrust took her breath away. Her body worked to adjust to the invasion, inner muscles clamping on his hot penis. His groan echoed hers. He pulled back and worked himself back in. "Just a little more, sweetheart. God, you're so hot."

She felt stretched to the brink of pain. "More?" she asked faintly.

A soft kiss pressed against her temple. Jace stood by her side and insinuated a hand between her and Marcus's body to pinch her nipple, twisting it harder than before. Surprised, she realized the slight tinge of pain only made her hotter. He leaned in close and whispered in her ear, "Just a few more inches. Let Marcus make you feel good, baby. Let him fuck you nice and hard, I promise you'll love it." Lust and excitement filled his voice.

She shuddered and made a conscious effort to relax, aided by the touch of Jace's hand on her breast. Marcus grunted and began thrusting with heavy lunges, each drive sinking him deeper inside of her, until the wall behind her vibrated in rhythm with their bodies.

All uncomfortable feelings gone, the need and hunger coiled inside her belly until she was straining, straining to reach the pinnacle. It was so close, just out of reach...

Devi sobbed her frustration as Marcus's thrusts grew shorter and harder, and as if she had spoken out loud, Jace responded and stroked his hand down her belly to open the tender folds that hid her clitoris, exposing it to the rub of Marcus's shaft. A few firm strokes was all she needed to implode, and she tilted her head back on a strangled scream, the walls of her vagina clamping down on the hard intruder within, milking Marcus's response as well. His heartfelt groan followed and he thrust up high inside of her, pushing her farther up the wall. His entire body tensed and stilled, almost-tangible heat rising off his shoulders as he came with teeth gritted.

As aftershocks of pleasure coursed through her body, she lifted her head. "That was ridiculous." The earth had moved, bells had whistled and all that jazz. Was this because of her relative inexperience? Was she supposed to do something right now and not just lay plastered to the very hard wall? She winced. Oh, there would be bruises tomorrow.

Marcus, his face buried in her neck, grunted, but didn't move, which made her feel a little better about being so very wiped out.

A masculine chuckle came from her right. She turned her head, a monumental feat. Jace tucked her hair behind her ear in an affectionate gesture that belied the heat in his gaze. He smiled a dark smile, and suddenly she didn't feel quite so tired anymore. "And just think," he mused. "That was just the first round."

# Chapter Four

Devi's eyes widened in apprehension, and Jace hoped, renewed lust. A flush covered her skin.

She was white hot. Perfect. Jace received a high from watching the pleasure in a woman's face, and he had never been with anyone as goddamned responsive as Devi. His dick was so hard it felt like he could drive nails. She kept trying to hold back her cries, but he and Marcus would break her of that habit soon enough.

Marcus slowly separated their bodies, and Jace could see the reluctance on his brother's face as he withdrew from her and removed her legs from around his waist. She wobbled a bit when she stood, and Jace steadied her with an arm around her waist while Marcus stepped back, holding onto the base of his condom. "Is there a bathroom around here?"

"The door to the right is a powder room." Her brows met as Marcus walked into the small bathroom. "When did he put that on?"

"While you were busy ogling me. Honey, that's the first thing you should insist on," Jace said.

"I-I guess I just didn't think." She looked deeply troubled by such an obvious lapse. Jace had the idea she didn't lose track of important matters on a regular basis.

"We're both clean, but it's a habit for us." Jace pressed a

light kiss to her forehead and pulled her closer. His hands coasted over the curves of her soft body. He couldn't touch her enough.

She stiffened a bit when she felt his erection pressed against her belly. "I'm not sure if I'm up for another bout of wall-pounding sex, Jace. Usually once a century is my quota for that sort of thing," she joked with apparent nervousness.

Poor thing. If this relationship worked out, he and Marcus would have her intimately acquainted with every piece of furniture and inch of wall in her home. "I prefer beds." True enough, though he didn't mind the occasional couch. Or car. Or bathtub. Or really anywhere a naked Devi happened to be, but why not let her figure that out on her own? Jace tugged at the strip of a shirt that still happened to be twisted around Devi's ribs, pulled it up and off and tossed it to the side. "How about a bout of headboard-pounding sex?"

She licked her lips, and a spark of shy excitement lit her face. "That can be arranged."

The water in the bathroom shut off. Devi looked over his shoulder and Jace knew the instant Marcus reentered the room by the flare of trepidation and hunger in her gaze. He placed a proprietary hand on her hip and urged her forward. "Lead the way, sweetheart."

Devi turned and walked ahead of them, casting a couple of nervous glances over her shoulder. He tried to give her a reassuring smile and make eye contact, but it was hard to pull off when the jiggle of her soft round bottom gleamed in the darkness. Unlike the rest of her honey-colored skin, her ass was almost white. Full in the manner of a Rubenesque goddess, his fingers itched to touch it, clench it, spank it. He wanted to feel it against his belly as he plowed into her from behind. A small groan came from Marcus and he grinned. Marcus appreciated a woman's ass even more than he did.

She led them through the living room and down a dark hallway, stopping at the first open door on the right. A large window dominated one wall, but the view faced a small backyard with a privacy hedge, so Jace didn't worry about voyeurs. Light streamed in from the moon outside, but he wanted more. He wanted to see every inch of her body, wanted to trace and kiss every curve. Jace turned to Devi. "Turn on the lights."

Despite the shadows, he could see the frown on her face. "I prefer the dark."

"We want to see you." Marcus stepped closer to her, and Jace knew her refusal would only arouse him more.

"Trust me, guys, I'd rather you not see every single one of my flaws."

"What flaws?"

She snorted. "If you have to ask that, then clearly the darkness is working in my favor."

"Devi, what did we talk about outside?" Marcus wrapped his arm around her and placed one hand on the curve of her ass.

"Right, you're going to punish me for—hey!" The sharp slap of flesh on flesh was punctuated by her cry. She pushed at his arm. "You hit me."

Marcus bent down and kissed her hard. "No, I just tapped you. And you have a lot more coming."

Jace could smell her arousal, see it in the way she tried to get closer to Marcus. "Where's the light, Devi?"

She looked at him, her eyes glittering. "The third switch by the door. Turns on the bedside lamp."

He was by the door in a second, and flipped the switch.

Soft light from the pink-fringed lamp on the bedside table flooded the room. Jace blinked. "Whoa."

"What?" Devi pulled away from Marcus.

"It's just so...female." A king-sized white canopy bed dominated the room, mounded high with a down comforter and pink and white pillows. The bureau and dresser were antique white with pink markings. Numerous bottles and assorted feminine things he couldn't begin to identify cluttered the surfaces. Lace curtains hung on the large picture window, and a window seat with teddy bears and stuffed animals sat under it. He frowned at those. They might have to negotiate the little creatures' presence if they were going to spend time in this room. Jace had a thing about plastic eyes, they creeped him out.

"I'm female." Devi placed her hands on her hips. Shapely hips. He took his time surveying her from head to feet and every single curve in between. He was a breast man, through and through, and hers were magnificent, full and heavy and topped by small brown nipples that looked as perfect as they tasted in his mouth. The rest of her was just as lovely. He lingered on her plush thighs and the intriguing little tuft of neatly trimmed dark curls shielding her pussy.

"Trust me, we can tell." Marcus gave her a lazy once-over. "And I repeat, what flaws?"

Some of the unease in her gaze diminished and her face lit up with a smile. "Well, if you can't see 'em, I'm sure as hell not going to list them for you."

"You know what I can see, baby? A fantasy come to life." Jace walked over to her and drew her toward the bed. He shoved the comforter to the foot of the mattress, hopped on and settled against the pillows, pulling her over him until she straddled his hips. "This whole frou-frou room is really giving me some nasty thoughts," he whispered in her ear.

"Like what?" she asked, breathless.

"Like we're the rude barbarians who have stormed the castle and captured the princess." Jace could feel the shiver that ran through her and hoped he was on the right track to tap into her arousal. "Of course, we'll make her submit to all of our"—he licked her ear—"perverted desires." He released her and pressed down on her shoulders in clear intention. "But first, I need the princess to take the edge off for me."

Her eyes widened with realization and nervousness. He waited with bated breath for her to call a halt, his hands on her shoulders but no longer exerting pressure. Instead, her little chin firmed and she met his challenge. She slid down his body with sinuous grace until she sat on her knees, the curve of her round ass sticking out. Tentative hands curled around the base of his cock and he arched up with a groan, gratified to finally, *finally*, have her touching him. She became more confident as she grasped his cock and milked it. He sank both hands into her dark curls and pulled her head closer until her breath gusted against the very tip of his cock. A small bead of pre-come dripped off the end and he shouted when she gave a tentative swipe with the flat of her tongue.

She drew back, her eyes startled. "Was that okay?"

Jace inhaled. "Honey, anything you do with your mouth and my dick is just peachy keen." Devi smiled, and a bit of feminine power lit her face. He pulled her back and she took him at his word. The first touch made his thighs tense. When she settled in to play, giving him tiny licks and strokes, he tightened his fingers in her hair to deliver a small shake. "Okay, enough teasing." She blinked up at him with such a patently false "who, me?" look, he almost laughed despite his arousal. "Suck me, princess."

Instead, she licked up the vein running along the underside of his cock and rimmed the tip.

He looked up to find Marcus standing at the foot of the bed staring down at her with an expression of dark desire on his face, fully aroused as if he hadn't practically pounded her pussy through the wall down the hall. Their eyes met and a silent agreement flowed. Jace spoke only for Devi's benefit, since Marcus was already climbing on the bed behind her. "I think our princess needs a little incentive to obey. Why don't you tan that sweet little ass until she understands how she needs to please us?"

Her eyes widened, and she attempted to pull away, but his hands tangled in her hair prevented her escape. With the first light tap of Marcus's hand, she jerked and whimpered. He hoped he had read her right, that she wouldn't call a halt. Sure enough, she opened her mouth and sucked him right in, her eyes promising sinful retribution.

Heaven. He closed his eyes in bliss. The soft suckling mouth, the sweet hands stroking in rhythm with her tongue and lips. The slaps of flesh on flesh.

He opened his eyes to find Devi's expression filled with confused pleasure. Marcus varied the rhythm and intensity of the spanks, so she didn't know what to expect from second to second.

"That feels good, doesn't it, baby?"

She whimpered in response and thrust back, raising her ass into Marcus's hand.

He nodded at Marcus who stopped his assault to reach underneath and press a finger inside of her. She moaned around his cock.

"She's even wetter than before," Marcus growled.

"Do you want to come?"

She nodded.

"Then you have to get me off first. Marcus will stop spanking that ass and we'll fuck you as soon as you do that."

Satisfaction filled him at the dazed compliance on her face. He tightened his grip on her hair and pulled her head down to meet his hips, forcing her to take even more of his cock. She gagged a little and he backed her off a bit and let her catch her breath.

Marcus took a break from his steady work on her ass to lean forward and speak in her ear. "If you want him to come, you need to swallow the next time he does that. That's the way we like our cocks sucked. You want to please us, don't you? So we can please you?"

She nodded vigorously. The next time Jace pulled her down, Marcus kept his hand on her neck, keeping her steady when Jace might have allowed her some breathing room. "Swallow."

She did, and for a second Jace popped past her throat's natural resistance, his dick caressed and massaged by the heat and wetness. He groaned and used his grip on her hair to pull her back. She drew on him hard with her mouth and whimpered when he almost popped out. No longer worried about scaring her, he screwed his hips in and out. He used her mouth roughly until he felt his come boiling in his balls.

"Shit, I'm going to come." He looked down. "Can you swallow it, baby?"

"Of course she can." Marcus slapped her ass again, a bit harder than before. "Can't you, Devi?"

She moaned and Jace took it in the affirmative, thrusting deep and holding her steady as he released down her throat.

When the last spasm of pleasure had left his body he watched as she released his cock with a wet pop and wiped at a smear on the corner of her mouth with the back of her hand. "Are you okay?"

She slowly shook her head.

Jace searched her face for any hint of disgust or remorse. "What's wrong?"

She crawled up his body until she straddled his hips. His cock was still hard and wet from her mouth.

"What's wrong?" She tossed her head and shot him a narrowed look that had him hardening further. "What's wrong is that I don't see anyone fucking me."

At her daring words, Devi could see Jace's post-coital glow flash back into lust. Marcus inhaled behind her. "Oh, honey, you need to watch what you say. Hearing dirty words fall out of those lips would just about drive any man insane."

The moment called for dirty words. Somewhere between the spanking and the take-charge way Jace had mastered her mouth, a key had been turned inside of her, and she felt wild and uninhibited. And empty. So very empty. She tossed a saucy grin over her shoulder and distantly wondered when she had become saucy. "So is anyone going to do anything about it? You've got me all worked up here."

Marcus smiled, a thin twist of his lips. "We're going to have to keep your ass red on a regular basis."

She shuddered in anticipation. How could she have known that a hard hand on her ass would turn her on so much? She had loved those slaps, had even arched her back and pushed back against Marcus's heavy hand for more pressure, which she was sure he couldn't have missed. Whatever slight stings of pain had been present had only worked her pleasure higher, the steady warmth of his palm adding to the rush of moisture in her vagina. Apparently, she was made for a little kinkiness.

"My turn for that sweet little pussy." Jace turned her around until she faced away from him, his erection still rock hard. She caught a glimpse of the foil packet Marcus picked up from the bed and handed to Jace, and then heard a tear. Jace traced one hand down her spine. A series of goose bumps launched in its wake. His erection nestled into the entrance of her soaked vagina.

"What about me?" On a less masculine man, the expression on Marcus's face might have been called a pout.

"You can have her mouth. Trust me, it's heaven. Unless..." Jace stroked a finger down the crease of her buttocks. He rested it against the small hidden opening. "Have you ever been fucked in the ass, Devi?"

She froze. No. And she hadn't planned that on the agenda tonight. How could she be so naive? Surely she should have realized that these two guys were very well versed in fucking a woman in every way possible. She shook her head and looked over her shoulder at him.

He inserted just the tip of his finger and pulsed it. She was surprised at the slight flare of pleasure but it didn't diminish her unease. A look of gentle understanding crossed his face. "We'll take you here eventually, but not tonight."

Not tonight? But all they had was tonight. Was he implying they would see each other again?

Before she could get too caught up in mulling over that, Jace rolled her over until she lay across the bed, her head at the very edge. He adjusted her body until she was on all fours. Without any preliminaries, he slammed into her from behind. Not that she needed any additional foreplay. While it had taken Marcus a few thrusts to seat himself inside of her, she was so wet and soft, Jace worked himself in with a single lunge.

She understood the position when Marcus stepped in front

of her, his cock at eye level. Without even being told, she sucked him in, reveling in his groan of pleasure above her. Who knew she had such an aptitude for this? Always an unpleasant chore before, now she felt proud that she could satisfy these two men in such a way.

She felt utterly full and stuffed, with Marcus's cock shuttling into her mouth and Jace screwing into her from behind. Their bodies were perfectly choreographed. She was always filled at one end or the other. Jace opened her folds so he could grasp her clitoris between two fingers, and within a few strokes, she was coming, her screams muffled by the cock in her mouth. With a rough groan, Marcus tore free from her grasp, his hand wrapped around his cock. He stroked it once, twice, before he came, his seed landing on her breasts where they hung beneath her. In her ear, Jace growled rough words of praise as he followed them into ecstasy. For one crazy second, she wished she could actually feel the spurts of warmth of his come inside her, muted by the condom.

She collapsed on the bed, the cotton sheets beneath her cushioning her body. Jace settled on top of her, his sweaty body a comforting warmth. Marcus flopped down next to them, his chest rising and falling in heavy breaths.

She dragged in a great lungful of air and blew a curl out of her eye. "Whew. I'm declaring a time-out before the next round."

# Chapter Five

The shaft of bright sunlight speared right through her closed eyes and into her brain. Devi screwed her eyes shut. Her inner thigh muscles ached, her limbs felt useless and her throat was sore.

From screaming. Amongst other things.

Her eyes popped open and she almost whimpered at the effort that move took.

“Morning.”

She rolled her head and took in Jace, his head propped up on one elbow. A lock of dark hair fell over his forehead, making him look rakish and carefree. He smiled widely, his teeth picture perfect.

She ran a tongue over her own fuzzy teeth and mentally calculated how long it would take her to work all the snarls out of her hair.

So. Not. Fair.

“Hey.” Devi eased up and clutched the sheet to her chest, unaccountably shy and awkward. They had spent the night going at it like rabbits, only stopping to sleep for a couple of hours or so at the end there. In all of her planning for this fling, she hadn’t rehearsed what they would all say or do the morning after. She guessed she had just figured the twins would poof out of her life the way they had poofed in.

Though maybe she had it half right. “Where’s Marcus?”

Jace shrugged, though a dark shadow moved in his eyes. “He’s an early riser. Probably already has coffee going.”

“Oh.”

“Devi, last night was amaz—oomph.”

She covered his mouth with her palm. “Please don’t say anything. I completely understand. You don’t have to make excuses. I totally went into this with both eyes open, knowing it was just for one night.”

His eyebrows met and he mumbled something.

“What?”

The little lines around his eyes crinkled and he removed her hand from his mouth. “I said, I don’t want it to be just for one night.”

“What?”

He pressed a hard kiss on her lips, and she was too stunned to protest her morning breath. He drew back and slid out of bed. “Why don’t you point me to the shower and we can talk about this over some breakfast?” With his back to her, he stretched his body up and groaned loudly. The powerful muscles in his back and buttocks tightened and released in a mesmerizing dance under tanned skin. “Devi?”

“What?”

He stopped stretching and looked over his shoulder. “Shower?”

Oh dear Lord, one threesome and her powers of speech were gone. “Oh yeah. The door at the end of the hallway is the guest bathroom.”

Jace placed his hands on his hips and turned to face her. The full frontal did not go unappreciated. Her eyes almost popped out of her head as they traveled the length of his body, which was bathed in bright sunlight. Did the man never get soft? Under her perusal, his erection thickened as if she touched it. She averted her gaze and cleared her throat. "Um, there should be some towels and shampoo and soap there. Let me know if you need anything."

"You know, maybe we could save some water and shower together."

Talk about temptation. Unfortunately, cavorting with two men all night long couldn't give her his kind of aplomb. She could probably get away with keeping the sheet around her for a bit, but he'd get suspicious if she didn't drop it once she entered the shower. All of a sudden, the soft lamplight she had objected to last night seemed far more preferable to the unforgiving sun filling the room. "Your conservatism is admirable."

"I'm very aware of my responsibility to the planet."

"But we'd probably get cleaner if we showered separately."

"There's clean, and then there's, well, raunchy shower sex." He held out his arms as if to offer his body.

*I don't want this to be for just one night.*

No, a girl needed a clear head to deal with such a curve ball. One didn't get a clear head by getting banged in the shower. More's the pity. "I think I'll stay in bed for a little bit longer." She faked a yawn and stretched her arms above her head. Only then did she realize how sore her muscles really were.

He gave in good-naturedly. Unashamed of his nudity, Jace plodded over to a small duffel bag sitting on her delicate pink vanity bench. He unzipped it and removed neatly folded Jockey's. She bit her lip as knowledge dawned. "How did that get in here?"

"Marcus brought it in from the car. We each keep an extra change of clothes in both of our trunks."

Of course. That's what all playboys must do. Stupid to feel hurt about that. Just then Jace glanced up. She tried to mask her expression, but she must not have been quick enough, because he straightened. "For the gym, Devi. See?" Jace reached into the bag again and pulled out a pair of running shorts. "I don't mind wearing my pants from yesterday, but it's nice to have fresh boxers and a T-shirt."

If it was stupid to be hurt over the thought of them being prepared for trysts, it was probably more stupid to be relieved that wasn't the case. Nonetheless, the knot of anxiety in her stomach eased.

Jace dropped the shorts back into the bag and walked over to a pile of clothes which lay on the floor. Devi blushed to realize her bra lay right on top. Marcus must have gathered the garments from the foyer. Jace picked up and shook out his dress shirt and slacks with a snort of disgruntled irritation. "The least he could have done was fold them neatly."

She rose up on her elbows and eyed the bundle of white cotton and grey twill in his hands. "I never buy any clothes that need an iron."

"Did I spend the night with a slave to the mass-produced wash-and-wear industry?"

"Guilty."

"If you want, I'll iron your clothes for you." He waggled his eyebrows. "I'll even wear nothing but an apron while I do it."

"Hmm, I can picture you in something pink with ruffled lace..."

"A manly apron," he corrected with haste. "One of those ones with a boiled lobster on it."

"I guess I can kiss the pearls and high heels goodbye, right?"

"Hey, look, lady, I'm kinky, but you're scaring me."

She was still chuckling when she heard his shower turn on. Devi jumped out of bed, gathered fresh underwear and clothes and headed to her attached bathroom.

Steam filled the small room and sank into her pores. She smiled to herself as she soaped up and thought of Jace in her pink guest bathroom. Bantering with him could become addictive. She didn't feel at all shy or awkward around Jace as she normally did around most men. Even Marcus, as intimidating as he was, made her feel relaxed and herself at some basic level.

*I don't want it to be for just one night.*

She ducked her head under the spray, allowing the water to wash away the suds in her hair and down her body. What had he meant? Did he want to keep seeing her? Having sex with her? By himself or with Marcus? Was Marcus in agreement? Where was he anyway? Had he left?

Maybe Jace just wanted to have another threesome. Like once more. Not multiple times. She shouldn't get her hopes up. Wait, was she hoping for more? Of course not.

"Argh!"

She grabbed the loofah and scrubbed her body until her skin grew pink. This was not supposed to have happened. An easy no-complications night now brimmed with complexities and potholes, and all thanks to a single sentence.

*This is what happens when you shine the light of day onto a fantasy. Way to go, Devi.*

Not that she would have changed a single second of last night for anything. For one night, she had lived her fantasy, and it had been amazing. She hadn't been frumpy or chubby, or heaven forbid, comfortable or sweet. She had been sexy. She stepped out of the shower, wrapped thick terrycloth towels around her body and hair and swiped her hand over the mirror to stare at her reflection.

With her hair slicked back, her features looked different, her eyes darker and bigger, her cheekbones more pronounced, her skin softer and clearer. As if her lovers' bodies had renewed her own.

She shook her head at such a fanciful thought but reached for her Victoria's Secret lotion instead of the generic store-brand stuff she normally used. She dropped the towel and slicked the cream over her flesh, the scent of jasmine permeating the room.

Even her skin felt different, the nerve endings more sensitized, tingling as she slipped a satin and lace bikini up her legs and snapped the front snap on her matching bra. *Thank goodness Rana gave me the matching set for my birthday.* Otherwise she'd be wearing striped orange briefs with a purple polka-dot bra. She really needed to invest in more lingerie.

Would she be needing it?

Yes. Even if Jace had been talking nonsense—which she was okay with, damn it—she liked the way she felt today. Like a new woman. No, like a real woman. Even if no one ever saw her nice panties, she would know. That would feel pretty cool.

She slipped a cute little yellow sundress over her head and sucked in her breath to pull up the side zipper. A much-needed improvement over her usual Sunday wear of faded jeans and oversized men's T-shirts. Devi ran a brush through her hair and studied herself in the mirror critically. Nice. Well, she would never be in her sisters' leagues, but the A-line skirt flattered her curves and the glow in her skin made up for a lot of flaws this morning.

Now, time to meet her men.

~ ❁ ~

Devi had a magnet on her dishwasher.

He should never have slept with her.

Marcus took a sip of his scalding coffee and studied the little happy hummingbird on the stainless-steel appliance. On one side, the hummingbird chirped "CLEAN", while on the other, it proclaimed "DIRTY". For some reason, the cheery domestic little magnet encapsulated everything that was different and wrong with them mixing it up with Devi. Hell, he'd never even seen any of their previous women's houses by the light of day. However, he doubted any of them had been the type to care what state their dishes were in.

He had tapped Jace awake around five, just when dawn had started to break, but his brother had merely shaken his head, drawn Devi closer and snuggled in to sleep. Marcus could read his thoughts without him even speaking. *You leave if you want, I'm staying.*

Marcus told himself he couldn't possibly leave, for the practical reason that they had come in one car and he didn't want to put Jace in the awkward position of having to call a cab in the morning.

*You could have called a cab.* Marcus winced. Well, duh. His practical reason didn't hold much water, especially since the truth was clearly evident. He didn't want to leave for the same reason he feared he saw in Jace—he was already halfway to smitten with the woman. That scared the figurative pants off him.

God, he wished he could have just jumped back into bed

and grabbed a handful of her softness for himself. But he'd never in his life slept next to a woman, and starting with Devi seemed like a monumentally bad idea. So, like an idiot, he spent a few sleepless hours on the too-short couch in the living room before stumbling in to brew a pot of his favorite gourmet coffee in Devi's state-of-the-art coffee maker.

Jeez, she would have to be a coffee connoisseur too, wouldn't she?

He glared at the hapless hummingbird and took another draw of his elixir.

Marcus didn't need to hear the footsteps behind him to know Jace had entered the kitchen. He could feel him. "Coffee's on," he grunted.

Jace didn't say a word until he had poured a large mug, taken a sip and sighed. He turned and surveyed the kitchen. "Wow."

"Yeah."

"It's very—bright."

Marcus took a look around the room. The stainless-steel appliances were all professional grade, worthy of someone who knew cooking, but the rest of the décor could only be called cheerful whimsy. Yellow gingham curtains hung over the large window and matched the tablecloth and chair covers on the little breakfast table, and daisies were everywhere. A vase of the fresh flowers on the countertop, magnets on the fridge, a cookie jar. If he didn't know better, he would have sworn Devi had exploded a can of spring in the room.

Jace cocked his head. "After seeing some of her rooms, I'm thinking our girl goes for the monochromatic effect."

*Our girl?* What, was she wearing their letterman's jacket? "Stop that."

"What?"

"Is she up yet?"

"Yup. And I even let her shower by herself. I think she's feeling shy again. She had a death grip on the sheet." Jace shrugged. "I didn't want to push her."

Marcus would have. The idea of Devi hiding her body bothered him, and as he had proved last night, he couldn't keep his civility around her. Then again, Jace generally had a softer touch where women were concerned. That was why they worked so well together.

"So what do you want for breakfast?" Jace opened the fridge. "We could go out, but I figured we'd do dinner out."

"Are you serious?"

"Well, I guess we could make dinner. It's just that we have such a limited repertoire, and I hate for her to feel pressured to cook for us constantly, you know?"

"I'm not quite sure what you're up to, but it needs to stop."

Jace closed the door and turned to him, his eyes round with surprise. "You *do* want her to cook for us? That's not really fair. She probably gets sick of it by the time she gets home."

Marcus felt like pulling his hair out. "Stop being obtuse. We need to leave."

"Now? Why?"

"Because that's what we do."

"Maybe that's not what I want to do."

"What about what I want? What about what she wants?"

A trace of something that looked like pity moved in Jace's expression. "You want to leave? Walk out on her without even saying goodbye? You think she would want that? That she wouldn't care?"

"We've done it before." They had, and he'd never thought twice or cared how the woman felt. A feeling close to shame wormed through him. Because no matter what tough-cookie act Devi put on, he knew she had never in her life had a one-night stand with one guy, let alone two. No, he didn't flatter himself into thinking her heart would break, but all of a sudden he didn't want to think of her experiencing that same feeling of emptiness that crept over him occasionally. "We should never have messed around with her."

"Why?"

"Why...?" Marcus battled the urge to shake his brother. "Christ, Jace. She's got a fucking magnet on her fucking dishwasher."

Jace leaned down and picked up the bird, his frown clearing as he turned it over in his hand. "Hey, this is ingenious. You'll never have to wonder if your dishes are clean. How clever."

Marcus gritted his teeth. "She didn't invent it, man."

"Still." Jace replaced the magnet. "I don't see what the big deal is."

"The big deal is she's not our type. I shouldn't have even agreed to this last night, but since I did, we need to minimize the fallout here."

"Why? Has she kicked us out? No. Do you want to leave?"

Marcus ran a hand through his hair. How could he possibly explain the fight-or-flight instincts running through his system? He felt trapped, like a cage was closing in behind him. "We never stay this long. I don't see what the point is. We're done here. I just—I think we need to go."

"So go."

The voice came from behind him. And it wasn't his

brother's. Aw, shit.

*It's no big deal, it's no big deal.*

Devi repeated the mantra to herself as she entered the room to walk purposefully to the coffee maker. She managed to avoid the eyes of both men. No easy feat—though her kitchen was roomy, the two giants took up a good amount of space, and then some. Jace wore his wrinkled pants from the night before, his spotless white T-shirt snug against his muscles, but Marcus wore only a pair of unsnapped jeans. His shoulders looked even larger than normal.

*You didn't even expect to see them in the morning.* So Marcus's words couldn't hurt her. They shouldn't.

They did.

At least in that stupid, sentimental part of her heart that had fluttered when Jace had said what he had in bed. Clearly, he had only meant he wanted to stay to enjoy a cup of her excellent coffee. Well, she owed them that for all the pleasure she received, she supposed. She poured herself a mug and turned to look at them, pasting a pleasant expression on her face.

Silence filled the room for a second as they both eyed her warily, as if she might fly into dramatic hysterics. Devi imagined what the three of them would look like to someone peeking in the window, standing like strangers in a stiff circle, while only hours before they had lain entangled in her bed in a human pretzel. "Well, thanks for the night, guys." She raised the coffee in a toast. "It's been real. Do you need directions?"

Jace set his mug on the counter with a clink and walked over to her to turn her around into his arms. He pulled her untouched cup away and placed it on the counter behind him before he encircled her waist with his arms and ignored the fine tension in her body. "Devi, sweetheart, like I told you, I don't want to go."

"I think Marcus would like to." She made a concentrated effort to keep her voice matter-of-fact, not whiny or petulant. She was proud of the final result.

A tortured sound came from behind her and Jace shook his head, sorrow in his eyes. "No, he doesn't. Or he would have left by now, not talked me to death." He looked over her shoulder. "Right?"

Devi gave a careless shrug. "You guys really don't need to stay on my account. Seriously, I didn't even expect to see you today."

"It's not just you." The words seemed torn from Marcus. Instead of looking at him, she stared fixedly at the hollow of Jace's throat. "It's—this whole place. You're such a nester. I don't want you getting any ideas."

Anger, unexpected and white hot, boiled in Devi's belly, until her pride outweighed her hurt. She turned around in Jace's arms, though he kept them wrapped loosely around her waist, to face Marcus. "Let me get this straight. You're worried that spending a civil breakfast with the two of you will have me picking out a china pattern? For what, a double-marriage ceremony? Give me a break."

"You don't get it. We never mess around with girls like you."

"Girls like me?"

"Good girls. You scream for a husband and kids and a white picket fence. We—I don't do that."

Oh God. She was sick, sick, sick of other people thinking they knew her. From her family to these men, they all had her pigeonholed as the sweet little girl just waiting in the hot kitchens for her prince to come. "Was I a good girl in bed last night?"

Jace's arms tightened. His tone rang with amusement. "If I could interject, I'd say you were a really good girl." He nuzzled her ear. "In fact, I'd say you deserve a reward."

Her lips twitched and her anger deflated a bit. Unfortunately for her blood pressure, Marcus doggedly continued. "That was your walk on the wild side. I get it. But now that it's over, you're either going to want to forget it happened or romanticize it out of proportion. That's all I was saying, that it was better to go before someone got to feeling uncomfortable."

She clenched her hands into fists. Better than clenching them around his neck, the conceited ass. "Look, I'm going to say this once, and please take it to heart or I'll be forced to brain you with one of my skillets: you don't know me. If you want to leave, fine. But don't you dare come up with some convoluted nonsense of how you think I'm going to potentially act."

"So you'd be okay with being our little fuck toy? Give me a break."

She must be depraved to feel a twinge—okay, a boatload—of arousal at his words. Devi raised her chin. "Maybe I would. Or did you ever think you'd be my fuck toy? Why can't I use you?"

Marcus opened his mouth, and then closed it again, and she was gratified to see him at a loss for words. She took advantage of his speechlessness. "I mean, let's face it, Marcus—my family's pretty conventional. One of my cousins raised eyebrows by marrying one white guy, so can you imagine what would happen if I brought two of you home to dinner?"

Marcus snorted and glanced away. "You have no idea how happy that makes—"

"To clarify," Jace interjected. "Devi, you'd be willing to have a repeat of last night?"

"Just...sex?"

"If you have no objections, I'd like to spend more time with you." His voice dropped an octave. "You're amazing. Last night was the best sex I've ever had."

"Me too." Marcus made the statement grudgingly.

"Seriously?" Jace she might have discarded as being charming, but she instinctively knew Marcus wouldn't lie. Wow. Go her.

"Yup. So what's the verdict?"

She couldn't help but look at Marcus. He sighed. "Yes. If Jace is set on this, I'm staying too."

He didn't sound particularly thrilled about it, more like resigned. Nevertheless, her libido woke up and did a somersault. Just having Jace in her bed a few more times would have been amazing, but both of them? Again? And again? And then, maybe, again? "Just sex." This time she stated it. No way could a long-term relationship ever come of this, so she would need to keep her heart well guarded. Could she do it? She didn't want to give them up just yet, so yes, she'd have to.

"How about we call it an affair?" Jace suggested.

"What's the difference?"

"You're too good for a wham-bam-thank-you-ma'am." Jace rubbed her arms. "You make me want to spend the day with you, whether we're having sex or not. I want to have a picnic or go to the movies without feeling pressured to whip out my cock."

She cast a droll look at Marcus. "I don't want anyone thinking I'm going to start nesting. So it'll be a short-term affair. Two weeks, max. But any party can walk away when they feel the need. No hard feelings."

"Do we have to put a time limit on it?" Jace asked.

She nodded. Oh yes they did. Any longer than a couple of weeks, and she wouldn't care what her family thought of her two lovers.

Marcus still seemed skeptical, but at least somewhat satisfied. "If you're okay with that, I guess I'd be stupid to complain, huh?"

Jace was slow to respond and she twisted her head around. "Jace?"

His gaze was enigmatic. "I only want what's best for each of us."

Now why did that sound evasive?

Jace lowered his head to brush his lips to hers. "I've never seen you in a dress. I love your legs."

She dismissed her suspicion and leaned back against his chest as though she had been doing so for years. Her legs were stubby in her eyes, but who was she to disabuse him of his notions? The tension eased a bit in her chest as she enjoyed the lingering kiss Jace pressed upon her lips.

His tongue swept her mouth, the taste of Colgate and the scent of Irish Spring flooding her senses until she forgot where she stood or who else existed in the room.

A rough growl reminded her a split second before Marcus slid his hands over her breasts and grasped her under her arms. He pulled her forward, breaking Jace's kiss and lowering his head. "She didn't even kiss me good morning, yet."

"You were too busy pissing me off."

Jace chuckled behind her. "You're losing your touch. Next time, maybe you should wake up with her the way I did. It might put you in a better mood, and you can get that kiss right off the bat."

Devi could sense some hint of underlying subtext to the words, but Marcus didn't reply to the goad, since his mouth was occupied ravishing her own. When he lifted his head, she made a soft sound of disappointment. He looked down at her and smiled. His dimples deepened, and that air of wariness he seemed to always carry vanished. With his guard dropped for a second, he looked far younger than he normally did. He glanced at Jace. "You're losing *your* touch, if you call that any kind of kiss."

A second later she was airborne. She yelped as Marcus lifted her and set her on the small breakfast table, pushing her skirt up to her waist in a smooth motion. He pulled her legs apart and stepped between them, his large hands clenching over the flesh of her thighs.

She lay back against the wood table and tried to relax as he knelt and kissed just above her knee. *You'll never be able to look at the breakfast table the same.* Oddly enough, the thought brought her some satisfaction. When had she ever done something so illicit in her kitchen? As his lips nipped and licked their way up her inner thigh, she felt her inhibitions at being bared to them in the morning light disappear in the midst of rising lust. The rip of tearing cloth brought her head up in shock. Marcus dropped the remnants of her panties to the side as Jace turned her head with a kiss. He pulled back to whisper against her lips. "Affair rule number one: whenever you wear a skirt around us, no panties. We'll take it as an invitation and we want you easily accessible."

She nodded, ready to promise anything. She caught her breath in a hitch as Marcus thrust two large fingers into flesh already overly sensitized from last night's use, curved them to hit the sweet spot buried deep inside her and dropped to his knees.

"Now here's a kiss."

Boy howdy, the man certainly knew his business. He brushed light kisses outside her vulva until she grew wet enough to drip, and then curled his tongue over the button of her clitoris to suck it hard. Just when she felt herself grow almost too sensitive to bear, he slipped his firm tongue inside of her and thrust. He spread her legs wider and settled in to feast.

Jace played at her mouth and massaged her breasts. The dual combination of both their lips and tongues and hands drove her to a quick and satisfying orgasm, the sound muffled against Jace's lips.

As she floated down to earth, she realized Marcus still knelt between her legs bestowing soft flicks against her sensitive flesh. She must have made some sound, because he withdrew with one last farewell nuzzle and stood. Jace broke off his kiss and stood as well.

Devi looked up at them from her position on the table. She couldn't bring herself to care about what kind of picture she made, with her skirt crumpled around her waist and sweat dampening her hairline. "That was...very nice."

For some reason, Jace found that hilarious and even Marcus cracked a smile. Jace slipped an arm beneath her shoulders and helped her to sit up and come to her feet. The dress fell down around her legs. While fully covered, she still felt bare without the panties and aware of her body in a way she normally was not. She looked down at her ripped underwear on the floor. "That was half of one of my only matching sets. You guys didn't even get to see me in it."

"Honestly, sweetheart, lingerie's nice, but we'd rather see you out of it than in it," Jace confessed and pressed a possessive kiss on her lips.

# Chapter Six

Devi slid her hand over the soft cotton covering Jace's hard stomach, delighted by the way his muscles tightened and jumped, and stopped at the fly of his slacks. The outline of his erection was clearly visible behind the fine twill.

He grasped her hand before she could continue and brought it to his mouth to nibble at her fingers. "As much as I'd love for you to make me feel 'nice' too, I'm starving."

Devi watched her finger disappear inside his mouth. "I really don't mind." And she didn't. She'd discovered she had a distinct aptitude for blowjobs. She loved the power high she received in controlling their bodies.

"I know, but we worked you hard last night. Let's eat and then we'll talk."

She tried not to feel too disappointed. He was right, her body wasn't used to such a sex-a-thon. "What do you want to eat? There's eggs, or I can make pancakes."

"What do you normally eat?"

"Honestly, I spend so much time cooking lunch and dinner, I usually just grab some cereal for breakfast."

"You're in luck, then, sweetheart." Jace pushed up his sleeves. "'Cause breakfast is one of the few meals I do know how to cook. Have a seat."

Marcus pulled out a chair and she sat down. Jace's movements as he put together the makings for an omelet were fluid and competent, and Devi found it captivating. Especially since, in her experience, men stayed far away from the kitchen. Though her father had passed away when she was barely fifteen, she couldn't remember him so much as picking up a spatula. After she reached adulthood, the men she'd dated just assumed she loved to cook so much she wouldn't want them to make anything for her.

Who knew domesticity could be so erotic? Maybe she would have Jace iron some of her clothes.

Marcus interrupted her musings. "Do you get the newspaper here?"

"Yeah. It should be on the doorstep."

He returned shortly with the bundled paper under his arm just as Jace set a refreshed cup of coffee in front of her. Marcus sat down and rifled through the newspaper, pulling a section out and placing it on the side of the table before settling in to read the front page.

The rustle of the paper, the crack of eggs, the steam curling over the lip of her coffee mug. What a completely domestic scene.

*Don't get used to it.*

No, she wouldn't. She rested a considering gaze on Marcus. However, she could enjoy the novelty of it, right? Tarek had been the last man to sit in her kitchen, over a year ago. She did mean sit, since she'd been the one scurrying around to fetch his food. At night she would scurry to fetch his slippers. Devi curled her lip. Just call her Ole Faithful. Thank God, her family and fate, she had seen the error of falling for that man.

Yet another reason not to get too comfortable around these heartbreakers. Double the drama when she got hurt.

As if he heard her deep thoughts, Marcus looked up at her. "Sorry, did you want a section?"

Devi shrugged. "Comics. And Lifestyle."

"Don't anyone touch my Sports," Jace tossed over his shoulder.

"I've already pulled it." Marcus rolled his eyes. "He hates getting a messed-up paper. It's a good thing I hate sports."

"So what do you read?"

"Finance, mostly. Comes in handy at work."

Devi paused mid-sip and lowered her mug to the table. "Oh. Right." How embarrassing. How could she not know what the man did for a living? Had Rana mentioned anything? She racked her brain. A lawyer? No, Jace was a lawyer. Anyway, lawyers didn't have anything to do with finance. Marcus watched her with an expectant look. She had a burning desire to know everything about him, but didn't want to admit her ignorance. Surely, Miss Manners would advise a woman to know what a man did for a living *before* she gave him a blowjob. "That's right. That...financial job you do."

His eyes crinkled and a slight curve graced his lips. Despite his lack of overt outward reaction, Devi could tell he was very amused. "I'm an accountant."

She laughed, but then paused when he didn't join in. "Really?"

"Yeah. Why is that funny?"

She thought of her family's accountant, a skinny, old balding man named Sol, and then looked at Marcus's tanned bare chest. "Ah, you don't look like an accountant."

Jace chose that moment to place their plates in front of them, heaped with fluffy omelets, crisp bacon and toast on the side. "Do I look like a lawyer?"

Devi studied him and considered the question carefully. "Yeah. You're sneaky."

Jace laughed but avoided her gaze, strengthening her suspicion from their earlier conversation that he was hiding something from her. "So, what are we going to do today?"

"Two choices," Marcus added.

Her thighs tensed in readiness but the soreness between her legs made itself known. Jace patted her hand. "We don't have to have sex—"

"Speak for yourself." Marcus raised the paper to hide his face.

"We'll be doing enough of that in the coming weeks," Jace said between gritted teeth. Devi wasn't sure if he was speaking to her or his brother. "What would you do if we weren't here?"

"Um, I actually needed to go to the mall—" A heartfelt groan came from behind the raised paper. Devi smiled. "Ahh, the universal male reaction to the mall scene. I was just about to say, I could skip it though and go sometime during the week. I just need to get a dress for my sister Leena's birthday party next weekend." She only had a couple of weeks with them. She didn't want to miss spending one of her few free days in their company just to complete a chore she didn't enjoy doing anyway.

Jace reached over with lazy presumptuousness and spread a pat of butter on the toast on her plate, which she tried to pull away. "I'm trying to avoid butter."

"Why? Fat's important."

Devi surveyed her plate. "I'd say I have enough of that right here." And on her butt too.

"Can't be too careful." Jace broke off a piece of bread and held it out to her.

She took it and the imp inside her had her swiping her tongue over the butter on his fingers. She delighted in the way his pupils dilated. "Hmm, maybe you're right."

For a second Devi thought he might haul her over the table, but the intense look on his face relaxed and he sat back. "You know, I need to pick up some stuff too. We can go to the mall first, and then maybe out to a movie and dinner. Have you tried Gormand's?"

Devi squinted. The last part of that sounded like fun—she had been dying to try the upscale restaurant for months, but the first part? She had just slightly more experience shopping with a man as she had with a man cooking, and she could easily say that experience had been horrendous. Trying to squeeze in and out of clothes that were not meant to be put on her body type was bad enough, but to have someone standing there, tapping their foot or glaring made it much worse. And with two of them there?

Another groan came from behind the paper, echoing her thoughts. Marcus flipped the top corner down and glared at them. "I can think of about thirty things I'd rather do than go to a mall on a Sunday. A partial lobotomy would probably rank up there."

Jace forked a bite into his mouth and true to his good manners, waited to speak until he swallowed. "Then don't come."

As much as she saw the good sense in that, Devi's heart skipped a little. She wanted to spend the day with both of them. She enjoyed Marcus's edginess as much as Jace's mellow personality. She shrugged and met Marcus's gaze. "We can do something else."

He frowned and looked back and forth between the two of them. "How long will you be?"

And so the toe tapping commenced.

"She's got to get a dress for her sister's birthday," Jace said as seriously as if she would be resolving the national healthcare crisis. "So, a while. Probably at least a few hours."

Marcus hesitated and studied her. "I'll come."

She narrowed her eyes at him. "You're not allowed to be a gloomy gus while we're there."

"Honey, you're dragging me shopping when I'd rather be rolling around the sheets with you. I can be any kind of gus I want to be."

Had he said a partial lobotomy? Marcus should have qualified it to a full lobotomy. Yes, he would rather have his brain removed than come wallow in this disgusting place of American consumerism.

They'd only just walked into the large revolving doors of the huge mall, but after navigating the packed parking lot and winding their way through crowds of giggling teenagers, Marcus swore he'd ground away part of his teeth enamel. Why would anyone want to frequent such a place?

Yet another reason to be grateful for Jace. His brother always handled all of this stuff for both of them. Sometimes all Marcus had to do was casually mention what he needed, and within a week it would be hanging in his closet. He would have felt guilty had he not known how much Jace genuinely enjoyed the whole clothes scene. Besides, his brother would be far more put out if he only wore the Walmart sweatpants he occasionally picked up with his boxers.

Hell, he wouldn't have even come today but he could tell

Jace wanted to spend the day out with Devi, and, well, he wanted to be around her too. He had known they would take a while. Could he be blamed for not wanting to putter around by himself when he could be enjoying Devi for the small amount of time they would be together? So what if this whole thing smacked of a date rather than a sex-only affair? They were all adult enough to see past that.

He hoped.

Like a stray pup, he trailed after the two of them as they strolled toward the major department store. To him, these stores always felt like high-end obstacle courses, the way a person had to wind and duck and dodge their way around the many corners. Marcus sighed in relief when he spotted a padded armchair tucked into a discreet corner of the ladies' department. He flopped into it to watch Devi and his brother in action. Clearly Devi wasn't used to shopping with an involved male participant, since she drew her lip between her teeth every time Jace made a suggestion or added an outfit to the pile in her arms. Jace knew his stuff and worded his opinions well, though—within a half hour, probably without her even realizing it, he had Devi agreeing with almost every word out of his mouth.

It became obvious pretty quick that Jace wasn't going to be happy until Devi had a whole new wardrobe. He recruited two salesgirls, and smelling money, the women scurried to fetch and hang the clothes they selected in one of the large changing rooms.

"No, not that color. Cobalt blue."

The petite salesgirl stared at Jace above the offering she had brought. "I'm not sure which..." she faltered.

Jace exhaled and walked to the far wall to fetch what he wanted.

As soon as he left, Devi released a long sigh and looked around until her gaze rested on Marcus. She tried a halfhearted smile. "You knew this was going to happen, didn't you?"

He shrugged. "I had a feeling. Don't tell him, but if there was a straight version of that old Queer Eye show, he'd be on it. He gets a kick out of dressing people."

She walked closer, and he appreciated the flex of the muscles in her calves. Her calves made him think of her soft thighs, though, and then what lay between them...

He shifted uncomfortably in the armchair. Erections and clothes shopping definitely shouldn't mix. She stopped in front of him. "Is there another chair?"

"Mmmm. Right here." A quick tug had her resting on his thighs. He shifted again to keep her delectable ass away from his eager cock. He didn't need any more encouragement. She gave a startled laugh.

"Ahh, how nice." Devi relaxed comfortably into his arms as if she sat on men's laps in public on a regular basis, which he highly doubted. "You know, I'm actually thrilled. I hate shopping for clothes, but this has been so much fun and I wanted to revamp my entire look anyway, from top to bottom. I'm so sick of wearing the same jeans. It's like Jace knows exactly what will look good on me."

"I know what would look good on you too."

"What?"

"Me," he whispered, and brushed a kiss against her lips.

"Ahem." They looked up to see Jace standing above them. "I need her back."

Devi stiffened in his arms. He looked past Jace to find the salesgirl frowning at them, no doubt wondering why this woman was snuggling her boyfriend's brother. He gave a mental sigh and released her. As soon as her warm weight left his lap, he wanted to tug her back.

Jace swept her up again, and he found it hard not to feel left out. Not that he wanted to be in that maelstrom of high-thread cotton, silk and satin, but he liked being the recipient of those megawatt smiles.

The emotion within him was so unknown he took a moment to examine it. Was he jealous of Jace? No. Had it been any other man, yes, but never his brother. He needed the connection their ménages gave him. Sometimes he felt so cold inside, he wanted to crack into a million little pieces. The sex grounded him, reminded him he wasn't alone. Through Jace, he could experience a tiny piece of what normal people felt and did.

In a new twist, he wanted to be involved here too, outside the bedroom. He wanted Devi to completely confuse the saleswomen and flirt and banter with him too. As ridiculous as it sounded, he wanted her to acknowledge that she was with both of them. Why? He couldn't say.

*Or you don't want to say.*

Whatever.

He slouched lower in the chair and glowered at the curtained-off fitting room that had swallowed up Devi. Jace had disappeared, probably to go find shoes or something. Marcus heaved himself out of the chair, and hands in his pockets, began to wander.

He wasn't really looking where his feet were taking him, so it was some surprise to find himself suddenly surrounded by yards of satin, lace and underwire.

Marcus reached out to handle a barely there bra of what looked like gossamer tissue. Devi said she wanted to change her wardrobe from top to bottom. Surely they couldn't forget the more intimate garments.

"It's called Wings of the Fairy. It's the newest design by Fredrico. Are you looking for a particular size?"

Marcus withdrew his hand hastily and looked down at the birdlike woman with the chirping voice. "Uh, no. I don't think this would support my, ah..."

"Wife? Girlfriend?"

"No!" At her startled expression he mentally kicked himself. Who else would a man buy lingerie for? Too bad short-term sexual partner was not a P.C. comment. "I mean, yes. My girlfriend." It didn't sound so bad. In fact, it sounded more comfortable than it should. "I need to pick out some things for her."

"Do you know her size?"

Finally, something in which he had complete expertise. "36D in bras—size seven panties." He stroked a finger along the satin underwear on the low table to his right. Panties with ties at the side were a definite must have. They would cut down on ripping. Maybe.

Unlike Jace and Devi, he could care less about labels, so he zipped through his shopping expedition within fifteen minutes, choosing a wide array of undergarments guaranteed to please all three of them.

He winced when the cashier read him the total. Why did women's underwear cost so much? Such tiny pieces of fabric shouldn't be so expensive.

"Your girlfriend's just going to love all of this," the clerk bubbled. Her face was flushed, no doubt from the charge she got from swiping his poor credit card. She misunderstood his flinch. "Oh don't be embarrassed. Lots of men come in here to purchase stuff." She nodded to a man browsing at the far end of the department. "That guy comes in every other week and buys his wife something. He says it keeps the passion going. So you're headed in the right direction. Keep it up." With a wink, she handed his card and receipt back to him.

He stuffed them in his wallet and gathered his four bags up, his gut churning. Keep it up? They only had a couple of weeks. What would he be keeping up?

Marcus looked down at the bags in his hands as he walked back to the ladies' department. The purchase had been a spur-of-the-moment decision, and now he questioned it. Did it smack too much of something a boyfriend would do? He had enjoyed imagining Devi in each ensemble, her café au lait skin framed by each piece. In reality, how many would he really get a chance to see her in?

"Where were you?"

The question jerked him out of his musings and he looked up to realize he had reached the ladies' department. Jace stood there, frowning in concern. "I figured you wouldn't be leaving your seat 'til we were done." Jace's eyes widened when he saw the bags in his hands. "What did you buy?"

Marcus shrugged in discomfort. "Nothing much. Just went by the lingerie department." He cleared his throat. "You know, to save us some time. Otherwise, we'd be spending another two hours there after this."

Jace's lips quirked, but he didn't comment. He nodded to the dressing room. "Devi's in there. If she needs an opinion on something, do something more than grunt, would you? I need to run over to the men's section."

Jace clapped him on the shoulder and headed off, leaving Marcus alone. He glanced around to make sure no saleswomen or customers lurked behind clothes racks and then walked straight into the dressing room. The floor-length doors to the closest two cubicles were wide open and empty. He could hear

Devi humming from the last little room.

He needed to put this affair back on track.

# Chapter Seven

The door opened behind her and Devi jumped and gasped. When the hulking man appeared in the mirror, she slapped both arms over her naked chest before she turned. "Marcus!"

As if he walked into ladies' dressing rooms on a normal basis, Marcus eased inside and set bags emblazoned with the store's logo to the side before he closed the door and locked it. "You should lock your door."

She glared at him. "I can see that. Do you mind? You really aren't supposed to be in here."

"And you really aren't supposed to be covering yourself up. Didn't we discuss this last night?"

"We can discuss it later. Now please get out before someone sees you."

"Hmmm. No, I can't do that."

"And why not?"

One minute he was two feet away and the next he had her pushed against the mirror, hands pinned to her sides, the glass cold against her bare back. "Because," he whispered close to her ear, "I think you're forgetting what our agreement was about. We haven't had sex in"—hc lookcd at his watch—"seven hours. What kind of affair is that?"

She gulped. Her spirits sank a bit with the reminder that

this was only supposed to be a fun sexcapade. In the past few hours she'd forgotten herself and had so much fun with them. She had half convinced herself she was really out shopping with her boyfriend. Boyfriends? Stupid.

However, that didn't mean she wanted to engage in a lewd public act. "Fine, we can go home and get in bed. Just give me ten minutes to get dressed and check out." She spoke in a reasonable and placating tone, as if to calm a troublesome child.

He looked down at her body, clad only in a flirty A-line skirt. "Are you wearing panties under that skirt?"

Her face felt hot. "I knew I was going to try on clothes, so of course I am."

"That seals it, then. You disobeyed me twice." He sighed, not bothering to hide the heat in his dark eyes. "So I'm afraid I can't wait to get home to punish you properly." He let go of her arms and unbuckled his wide leather belt.

Despite her fear, her nipples hardened to ready points. His gaze catalogued every inch of her arousal, missing nothing. Still, she tried again. "Marcus, please be reasonable. We cannot screw here. Someone could see."

"We're not going to fuck. Where would the punishment be if I fucked you? I get my dick inside of you and you come like the Fourth of July."

His jean buttons slipped out of their holes with tantalizing slowness, until the bulge of his erection filled the widening V. He pushed his boxers down, and his cock was in his hand, hard and large and intimidating. He curled his hand around it and stroked roughly until the mushroomed head emitted a small drop of fluid. Devi licked her lips. "On the other hand," he continued in a low voice, "you love to suck cock, don't you? It makes you as hot as I get when I go down on you. Don't be embarrassed, baby. You don't know how happy that makes us. You're one in a million. So that's your punishment. You get me off here...and then wait for yours." He pulled her unresisting hand to his penis and wrapped it around himself. The flesh was hot beneath her fingers, his pulse pounding.

"But what if someone comes in?"

"You'll just have to hope no one comes in, if that bothers you. The faster you get me to come, the better it'll be, right?"

He showed her how he liked it, tightening her fingers, lubricating her hand over each pass of his tip, until his shaft was wet and shiny with come and her hand slicked over every inch. He shifted until he could tilt his head back against the mirror and closed his eyes.

"Miss?"

Her hand froze on his dick, and her startled gaze met his heated one. Impossibly, he hardened even more. "Yes?" she said faintly.

He rested both hands on her shoulders and began a steady downward pressure. Devi shook her head frantically. His eyes narrowed and threatened if she didn't obey. *On your knees. Now*, he mouthed.

"How are you doing in there?"

She should have been too horrified to move. Instead, her stomach clenched in arousal. God, was she a complete pervert? "Fine." She responded to the pressure and sank to her knees. Marcus tangled one hand in her hair and grasped his cock with the other. He pulled her closer and stroked her cheek with the velvety-soft head.

"Your boyfriend just left. He said he'd be right back." She sighed, naked envy in the sound. "He is so cute, if you don't mind my saying so. His brother wouldn't happen to be single, would he?"

His brother currently had his cock pressed against the seam of her lips. “Um, no.”

Marcus took swift advantage of her open mouth and thrust in, catching her off guard. He made a few shallow thrusts before tightening his fingers in her hair and forcing a deeper penetration. The head caressed the back of her throat, and the walls spasmed around his hardness. He exhaled, just a breath of noise, his eyes almost black, fierce, as he stared at the length of his cock shuttling between her lips.

“...so sad.” A light laugh. “Well, you’re a lucky lady to have just one of them. Holler if you need anything, okay?”

She was even luckier to have them both. Marcus drew her off his penis long enough to answer. “Thanks.” The light footsteps faded away. “Lucky, my foot,” she mock grumbled.

He tugged her hair. “You love it,” he whispered.

God help her, but she did. He drew her mouth back to his penis and she became lost in the ferocious power of his need. No longer content with teasing thrusts, he sank both hands into her hair and held her steady for his taking, long, fast thrusts to the back of her throat. All she could do was hold on and concentrate on swallowing when necessary to fight her gag reflex. That had the added benefit of driving his arousal even higher, as he took her mouth harder and rougher.

Marcus shifted to the side, and she followed, turning her body and head. “In the mirror,” he whispered, and stroked the side of her cheek. “Look.”

She obeyed, and her stomach clenched with need at the sight that greeted her. He was fully dressed but for the hardness that glistened with her saliva as it slipped in and out of her mouth. Meanwhile, she looked like a complete sexpot, hair tousled every which way, her mouth reddened and stretched with his fucking, her eyes dilated with desire. Her skirt pooled over her bent knees in deceptive demureness, while her bare breasts shivered with every forceful thrust of his hips.

As if he read her mind, he reached down with one hand and cradled her breast, his hand looking very tanned against flesh that never saw the light of day. His thumb stroked in circles over her brown nipple, the tip tightening to the point of pain. In his profile in the mirror, she could see the sly grin that curled his lips as he compressed the nipple between his thumb and forefinger at just the right pressure that shot bolts of sensation to her vagina.

Watching intensified everything she could feel, the stroke of his cock in her mouth, his hand in her hair, his fingers on her nipple, until she squirmed on the rough carpet of the dressing room. She needed just a couple of strokes, a touch, and she could come and release all of that burning pressure inside of her. She closed her eyes and released his hips to press the heel of her hand down on her pussy. She was so close, she could even bring herself off without touching herself under her clothes. Would he give her other nipple the same attention he gave its twin?

In the next breath, it all stopped. His cock slipped from her lips, his hand fell away from her breast. She whimpered and opened her eyes in disbelief.

His chest rose and fell, and his cock looked ready to burst. "You don't ever touch yourself without my permission."

Oh please. "It's my body," she gritted out.

"No. For two weeks, it's mine."

She really was a pervert, since his statement only made her hotter. She tried a different tactic. "Please, Marcus?" She leaned in and pressed a soft kiss to the straining tip of his penis, delighting in the catch of his breath. She didn't even care if anyone came in, if anyone heard them outside. She could deal with mall security after she got off. Nothing was more important than that in this moment.

"Don't try to sway me." He raised an eyebrow, and the arrogance just about melted the panties right off her. "Or you're going to be without relief for a long time."

Before she could argue, he put his hand on her head and thrust into her mouth again. "Or maybe you can convince me otherwise. Show me how good you are at sucking my cock, baby." She sucked hard, until her cheeks hollowed and caressed his cock with every thrust. "Yessss," he hissed.

He came silently, with only a soft exhale of sound between clenched teeth. She swallowed every drop he gave her and kept sucking gently as he softened between her lips. Marcus finally leaned against the wall and disengaged with a pop of suction, her mouth was so tight.

He ran a hand over his face. "Fuck. That was amazing."

She squirmed, feeling the wetness that had trickled down her thighs. She swiped the back of her hand over her mouth. "I'm glad you think so."

Marcus smiled down at her. "Don't disobey, and you won't have to deal with the consequences."

"You and I both know that was a convenient excuse, nothing more."

He gave a shrug and tucked himself back in. She almost mewled when he zipped up that amazing cock. "Get dressed. And maybe we can take care of you."

Marcus walked to the door and reached down to pick up his bags, which she frowned over. Marcus didn't seem like the type to purchase quite so much. "What's in those bags?"

His back stiffened. "Um, just some lingerie. I figured if we were ripping it from you, we should be buying it."

"Wow. That was...very thoughtful." He looked as though he had gone overboard, though, to pay her back for one pair of panties.

"Hell, it's more for us than you. We're the ones who'll be seeing you in it."

"Oh, well. Thanks anyway."

"Yeah. Whatever."

"Don't let anyone see you leaving here."

He snorted, but stole out on silent feet. Devi waited for shrieks of feminine outrage, but a full minute went by with nothing but the hum of the air conditioner and the discreet overhead music. She sighed and leaned against the mirror, cold against her overheated body. God, they were lucky no one had come in. What had she been thinking? They'd practically been speaking in normal tones there for a bit.

She turned her head to look into the mirror and her eyes widened. Well, hell. Devi Malik, shy little mouse, would never have done what she had done. But the topless jezebel sitting on the floor would have no problem blowing her lover in a public dressing room. In fact, she had almost lifted up her skirt—that still had a tag on it, for crying out loud—and begged him to take her right there for all the world to see.

She licked lips that felt stretched and swollen, searching for a small smidgen of shame. No, all she could feel was unfulfilled and empty. Dear Lord, surely Marcus wouldn't make her wait too long for satisfaction. Right?

Jace saw Marcus slipping from the dressing room out of the corner of his eye and breathed a silent sigh of relief. He didn't know how long he could have kept chatting with the bubbly and irritating salesgirl to keep her away. Thank God they had been relatively quick, and it was an unusually slow shopping day, or he would have had to chat up every matron and teenager who had looked remotely interested in trying clothes on.

Devi came out not five minutes later with a pile of clothes draped over her arm. As she walked closer to him, he noticed little details, like the mess of her black curls, her swollen lips, the flush on her high cheekbones and the glitter in her black eyes of unappeased desire.

"I'm going to kill your brother."

He choked back a laugh, understanding by her crisp words that humor would not be appreciated. She sailed by and thumped the armful on the counter.

"Are you hungry yet? If not, we can walk around the mall for a while..." Jace shut his mouth when she wheeled around. The incendiary look she shot him had his cock sitting up to take notice.

"I want to go home right now." She turned back to the cashier and fumbled her credit card out of her purse. Jace rocked back on his heels. He would have paid, but he knew she would have a problem with that. That was why he had already purchased those clothes she had deemed too expensive and stored them in the car. And a few pairs of shoes. And the odd handbag or two.

Jace didn't mind at all that Devi wasn't a fashionista. There shouldn't be more than one of those in any relationship. He loved dressing her to show her off, watching her confidence bloom. He had carefully steered her toward clothes that would let her natural beauty shine through, but still remain comfortable and suit her style.

Things were going well. The two-week time limit Devi had placed on their affair had thrown him there for a bit, but he remained fairly confident he could win both of them over. No way would Devi allow any man to stake his claim on her in a public dressing room unless she was too enthralled to complain. Though physical desire wasn't love, it was something workable.

Jace watched her jerky movements as she stuffed her wallet back in her purse and felt a shot of fear at the thought that his brother wouldn't come over to his way of thinking. He had just experienced one of the best nights and days of his life, thanks to the woman in front of him. Would he be able to say goodbye to her if Marcus remained stubborn?

He couldn't have a relationship with her by himself. The complex ball of guilt and love that had bound him and his brother together in the nightmares of their teenage years had pretty much destroyed any chance of a normal life with their own women.

But, God, what he wouldn't do to come home to Devi at night. Her softness and sweetness were like a balm to his soul. He walked up behind her and inhaled her unique floral scent. "Ready?" Jace frowned at the soft chiffon skirt the salesgirl slipped into a bag. "I thought you didn't like that skirt?"

If possible, her tan skin flushed a little deeper. "I changed my mind. You were right. I have to buy it now."

Jace suppressed another smile. Something illicit must have happened while she wore it. Of course Devi would feel responsible for purchasing it, even if she never touched the skirt again.

She grabbed hold of both of her bags, and he promptly relieved her of them and held out his crooked arm. She slipped her hand through it. Her short unpainted nails clenched into the fabric of his shirt. "I really need to get home," she said in a low voice.

He pressed a kiss to her soft curls. "Don't worry, I'll take care of you. I think Marcus is already at the car."

Devi released a shaky sigh. "Thank God."

The sun shone off the silver of Jace's car as they approached it, like a beacon to Devi's sexually strained nerves. Every step rubbed her sensitive thighs together and she was all too aware of the points of her nipples under her dress and bra.

Marcus already sat in the driver's seat and cranked the engine as soon as he spotted them. Devi shook her head when Jace opened the passenger door and grabbed his hand instead. Within seconds, she straddled him in the backseat. He was laughing, but sobered when she fastened her mouth on his and released her pent-up need into the kiss.

His tongue came out to duel with hers and he slid a hand into her hair, tilted her face to the side and held her still for his taking. She followed him when he tried to disengage and nipped at his full lower lip.

"Drive," Jace growled, the sound muffled by her mouth.

Distantly, she heard the rumble of the motor and the vibration of the car as they drove, but all she could think about was the hard cock between her legs and Jace's strong arms wrapped around her as he kissed her out of her socks. If she had been wearing socks, that is. Which thank God she wasn't, because it would just be one more thing to get out of.

Jace's hand rasped the skin of her thigh as he drew her skirt up. He paused and drew back when he reached the barrier of her panties. "Don't start with me," she snapped when he opened his mouth. "There was no way I was going to try on clothes without panties. Your rules can't always work."

A slow smile curled his lips. "Our rules always work. But I guess you've been punished enough." With a quick tug the panties disintegrated and he tossed them to the floor of the car.

*And another one bites the dust,* Devi thought with an inward sigh. Hadn't these guys ever heard of stepping out of underwear?

All thoughts of panties flew from her mind when Jace clenched her bare buttocks in his hands and pulled her up so the distended zipper of his slacks fit right into the lips of her pussy. The fabric seemed rougher than it should against her tender folds, and he dragged her up and down his length. Jace kept one hand on her ass and swiftly pulled at the bodice of her dress to free her breasts. He growled in frustration when he encountered her bra before he tugged that down so her breasts were offered up to him as if on a shelf.

Jace accepted the invitation and leaned in, latching on to her nipple and sucking strongly. Devi reached between them to unfasten his pants, feeling desperately empty. The button and zipper were stubborn, though, and Jace made no move to help. She sobbed in frustration. "Jace, please..."

He nipped at her and then soothed with his tongue. "Please, what?"

"I-I need you."

"Say it." He smiled against her nipple. "And use the bad word."

"Please...fuck me."

Just like last time, her cursing worked like an impetus, and he let go of her to fumble in his pocket. She saw a glimpse of foil, heard his zipper, a tear, and then he was guiding her back.

"Oh...God." Her head fell back as he held her hips steady and lowered her onto the upthrust length of his cock. Once he seated himself, he stopped and she opened her eyes to see him gazing at the point where they joined, her dark curls meshing with his more wiry body hair. He moved his hips just a fraction of an inch deeper, hitting a spot they had discovered during the excesses of the previous night.

She gasped and clenched her fingers into his shoulders. “Oh, please, harder.”

He kissed her, pushing her until her back met the passenger seat behind her. With his hands brutally tight on her hips, he slammed into her again and again, going deeper each time, faster until she felt as though he was just another part of her body.

She writhed in his lap, but as wonderful as the stimulation felt, it just wasn’t enough to make her come. She heard a mechanical whir and was startled to feel a large hand on her cheek, turning her head. She met Marcus’s gaze and realized he had shoved his seat back until it met the backseat. “Driving?” she gasped.

“We’ve stopped.”

She caught a flash of green outside the window and spared a moment to hope Marcus had found a secluded spot. Then again, she couldn’t care less if he had parked on the side of the freeway. He leaned sideways and captured her nipple in his mouth. Each tug made her womb contract.

Marcus’s rough fingers found her hard, swollen clitoris. He scraped her nipple with his teeth before letting it go. “Don’t you want to come?”

She rolled her head from side to side against the butter-soft leather against her back, the agonizing tension unbearable. “Yes!”

She felt rather than saw him nod. Jace stopped thrusting and held her clamped to his body. One of Jace’s hands coasted down the crease of her buttocks and she tensed in confusion. He followed the line until his finger circled the rim of her anus. She pushed away from his hand, whimpering in fear, but they brought her back.

"Relax, Devi." Marcus's voice was so authoritative, it cut through her haze of need and confusion, and she focused on his face. "You know we won't do anything you won't like." True enough. Everything they had done so far, even the dressing-room incident, had brought her nothing but pleasure. She relaxed a bit in their arms as Jace dipped his finger into the moisture of her pussy and then slid back to her ass and slowly pushed at the opening.

She jumped when just the tip of his finger popped through the opening. The sensation was unique—a slight burning, but no real pain. Actually, the fullness felt rather intriguing. Devi squirmed a bit to experience a deeper penetration but stilled when Marcus pinched her clit between his fingers.

"Feels good?" He rubbed the little nubbin with his rough finger and Jace started thrusting with shallow strokes.

"Answer him, Devi." Jace's tone was hard, no longer his usual mellow self.

"Yes."

"You like my finger up your ass?"

"Yes, more, please." Who knew she would beg for more?

"Not now," Jace panted. "You'll tear."

She bore down on him anyway but stopped in shock when Marcus delivered a light slap to her clitoris, sending fireworks exploding across her nerve endings. She met his fierce gaze. "Don't disobey. We'll give you more later." He leaned in close, his whisper brushing over the sensitive skin of her ear. "I'll take you to this store I know about, Devi. I'm going to buy you a butt plug. Will you wear it for me? That way you'll be nice and ready when we finally fuck you here. We're both going to fuck that tight little ass, and then you're going to take us together, one of us in your ass, the other in your pussy." His voice was dark with anticipation. "You'll never feel anything better. Would you like that?"

To be filled from one end to the other. She couldn't think of anything better. Jace's thrusts had picked up speed, but Marcus kept his finger light on her clitoris. "Yes," she moaned. "Anything you want."

"Good girl. Come *now.*" He pressed down hard on her clitoris and Jace shoved as deep inside of her as he had ever been. The tension inside her exploded, the walls of her pussy clamping on Jace's cock. He groaned long and low, his shoulders tensed, and she knew he was coming as well. The knowledge set off another climax, not as intense as the one before, but no less satisfying.

She slumped against Jace. He gently pulled his finger free of her ass, and she felt rather empty. What would it be like to have both of them inside of her at the same time?

She wasn't quite as opposed to the idea anymore.

The rumble of Jace's chest beneath her ear roused Devi into looking up. His face was filled with mirth. "What's so funny?"

He smiled. "I was just thinking—this is probably the best mall trip Marcus has ever experienced."

# Chapter Eight

"*There* you are."

Devi stiffened, and then made a conscious effort to relax her shoulders. Damn it, she'd hoped to have more time before she had to encounter Rana. She'd rushed straight from her bed to work, with a quick pit stop in the shower. She didn't exactly look as unruffled and put together as she'd hoped.

Well, it couldn't be helped now. Devi shut off the faucet of the utility sink and grabbed the towel. "Hey."

Heels clicked on the tile. They stopped directly behind her. A pregnant pause filled the room as Devi concentrated on drying every ounce of moisture on her fingers.

Rana broke the silence. "Well? Is that all you can say to me? I've been dying to talk to you."

"We talked last night."

"Yeah, after I called you all day and threatened to come over. And you didn't *talk* to me. A quick 'hi' and 'see you tomorrow' does not qualify as a talk."

"I was just tired. I told you."

A pause. "You are physically all right, right? They didn't hurt you? Because so help me God...what did they do? I knew it. I knew you weren't ready for this. I shouldn't have done this. Leena is going to kill me. Are you bruised? Are the bruises under your clothes? Let me see them. We have to get you to the hospital. Oh no, your hair's wet. You showered. You aren't supposed to shower!"

Devi dropped the towel and spun around. "Holy crap, Rana. Get a hold of yourself. No one hurt me."

Rana took a deep shuddering breath and pressed one manicured hand against her heaving chest. "Are you sure?"

"I think I'd know."

"Are you experiencing some sort of weird victim's guilt?"

Devi rolled her eyes. "No."

"So, you're okay?"

"Of course. Why wouldn't I be?"

"You sounded stiff yesterday. Did everything go as planned?"

"Um, sure."

Rana scrutinized her for what felt like an eternity. Devi fought not to flinch, blush or fall to the ground in a blubbering mess of rattled emotions. She must have done a good job of pretending nonchalance, because Rana's worry melted into a sly knowledge. "So..." she purred, and cocked a hip. "Did baby sister enjoy her one night of sin?"

Oh no, she couldn't do this. Couldn't even begin to explain how they hadn't been able to end it at one night. Rana would leap right back into overprotective mode. "I, ahh..."

"What was it like?"

"Well..."

"Was it amazing?"

Rana crowded closer. The sink bit into the small of Devi's back. Talk about a rock and a hard place. "I'd really rather not..."

"How big...?"

"Rana!" Devi sidestepped and tried to put some distance between them. "If you don't mind, I don't want to discuss this."

Rana pouted. "Come on, Devi. I've never spoken with a girl who I knew for a fact slept with those two. Throw me a bone here. Ha! Sorry, everything's gonna sound like an innuendo. Bone."

Devi tried to control the involuntary twitch in her eye. She'd rather not think of the parade of other women who might have come before her through the Callahan's revolving doors.

Yet another reason to question her judgment in getting involved in this affair.

"Do they look the exact same naked?"

Devi huffed an irritated breath. Thank God they were the only ones in the room. Rana had no shame. She would have felt as justified grilling her in front of witnesses. "I need to start cooking. I do not want to discuss this with you. I will not discuss this with you. So you can ask questions 'til kingdom come, but I am not going to tell you a single detail about Saturday night." Or Sunday morning. Sunday afternoon. Sunday evening. Oh, and the last time Jace had slipped his penis inside of her had been well after midnight. So add Monday morning to that list as well. No, she couldn't tell Rana about any of those monumental experiences.

"Well, hell. Fine."

"Good." Devi pulled out a covered bowl from the fridge and set it on the counter. She opened an airtight container, scooped out a bit of flour and sprinkled it on the clean cutting board.

"Devi."

She looked up.

"It was good, right?"

Had she not known her sister so well, she would have missed the shadows of guilt and pleading in her eyes. Affection and understanding coursed through her. When would Rana understand she didn't need to make anything up to her, that she didn't hold the past against her? "Yes," she said gently. "It was exactly what I needed. Thank you so much."

Rana let out a breath and the heretofore unnoticed tension in her body dissolved. "I did okay, then."

"You did great. Now, a couple of people are already seated out there, so let's get to work."

Devi managed to keep the slight smile on her face until Rana left the room. She turned on the range and placed a cast-iron skillet on top of it. While it heated, she peeled the cover off the bowl in her arm to reveal the huge ball of dough Asha had set to soak last night. Flatbreads were a staple of every meal they served, and she loved Monday mornings, when their business was slow enough that she actually got a chance to enjoy the process of putting together each part of the meal. Today, especially, she relished the chance to pound out her misgivings.

She kneaded the ball to check its consistency before she twisted off a walnut-sized section and rolled it between her hands.

The unease churning through her could be laid to rest directly at the twins' feet. She'd woken up alone this morning. Well, granted it had been late, almost ten, which gave her just a half an hour to get to work. She wasn't an idiot—of course they'd had to get up early and go to work. They'd had to go home and get some clothes too.

So, intellectually, she had known she would wake up alone today. She'd needed the sleep, and it had been considerate of them to allow her that luxury. In their defense, Jace had left her a sweet note on her pillow. And another one on her bathroom counter. And a sticky taped to her cell phone to let her know he'd programmed both of their numbers into her phone.

Marcus hadn't left her any messages.

Dough oozed between her clenched fingers, and she sighed at the waste of mangled yeast. Devi rolled it back into a neat ball and patted it down on the flour-strewn board. With her rolling pin and a few efficient strokes, she flattened it into a circle.

Well, of course Marcus hadn't left her any messages. Had she really expected any differently? The man couldn't even sleep with her. She'd woken in the middle of the night when he had slipped from their warm bed, presumably to go sleep on the couch again.

She'd never been a needy girlfriend. Or lover, that is. Tarek had once gone almost two weeks without contacting her, and they'd been actively dating at the time. This shouldn't even faze her. Granted, that relationship had been riddled with problems, so it probably wasn't the best comparison, but still.

She picked up the thin circular dough and placed it on the skillet. Small white bubbles immediately appeared on the surface of the *chapatti*. Ignoring the spatula, she used her fingers to flip it over. In another minute, with a practiced move, she removed the pan and dropped the bread directly onto the gas burner. Within ten seconds, the *chapatti* puffed full of air, and Devi picked it up, again with the tips of her fingers, and dropped it into the warmer on the counter. Leena hated her method of making the popular flatbread, claimed it was dangerous, both to Devi's fingers and as a fire hazard. But pan-frying alone couldn't give the soft tortillas that flame-cooked taste. Besides, after years of making the side dish, the tips of Devi's fingers were completely desensitized to the heat, and she was always careful. Her mind might wander, but she knew what she was about.

She pulled off another piece of dough. Devi had no right to demand Marcus sleep with her. Talk about selfish. Jace had slept with her, and for a short-term affair, that was already going above and beyond. Actually, if they hadn't been so exhausted yesterday after their sexual excess, maybe they would both have just left.

Maybe tonight, after they were finished with each other, they would leave. Or she would leave, if they decided to go to their place. Maybe they wouldn't even meet tonight. After all, Jace had written he would call her later. Devi stared at the *chapatti* puffing up on the open grill. Maybe he was going to call her to tell her the deal was off.

As if she had conjured him up, the cell phone in her apron pocket buzzed. With shameful haste, she grabbed for the phone, unmindful of the butter that smeared across the pink surface.

Jace.

Yup, there was his name, right across the display. Okay, good. Check off "not a liar" under his personal list of accomplishments. She took a deep breath and answered the call. "Hello?" To her everlasting gratefulness, she managed to keep her tone breezy and unconcerned.

"Hey, sweetheart." The warm velvet honey of his tone sent all her little nerve endings into a happy dance. Just like that, all of her breezy unconcern went out the window, and she found it difficult to say anything.

"Devi?"

Her voice returned. "Um, yes, hello."

"How are you doing?"

Devi wedged the phone at her shoulder and wiped her greasy hands on the apron, which she probably should have attended to first. “Fine. I’m just—oh my God!”

“What?”

Devi let the phone drop to the floor and flipped the charred *chapatti* off the burner. Something else she should have attended to first. She waved a towel at the small amount of smoke the potential fire hazard generated. Thank God she had noticed it or Leena would have more reason to bitch about her method of cooking.

Not to mention the tongue-lashing she would have gotten for talking on the phone while cooking. Normally she kept the phone in her purse in the office. Family businesses had rules too. She’d just been hoping Jace would call...

Aw, crap. She sighed just as the phone buzzed loudly against the tile. He must consider her a massive ditz.

She crouched to pick up the phone. “Hey.”

“Did something happen?”

“No. Of course not.” She gave another halfhearted swipe at the residual smoke. “You know, just hanging out in the kitchen. What’s up?”

She thought he might call her on her more-than-obvious bluff, but he let it go. His voice became more intimate. “Just wanted to make sure you were doing okay.”

“I said I was fine.”

“Physically, I mean.”

She puffed her cheeks up with air and tried not to let her face heat. “What is up with everyone asking that today?”

“Who else would ask you that?”

“Never mind. Yes, I’m fine.”

“No soreness?”

Hell yes, soreness. However, she'd participated heartily in creating that soreness, so she couldn't exactly complain about it now. "Nope."

"Well, great. I was just sitting here, thinking of how rough we were on you." His tone deepened. "And then I got hard, remembering how you took it. How you loved it. How you arched your back, pushing your breasts up for my mouth."

Devi opened her mouth, but no words came to mind.

"Remembering the feel of your tight little cunt around me, like a hot little mouth sucking on my dick."

Holy moly, these men were potent. "Are we having phone sex?" she blurted out.

Jace chuckled. "Not yet. I was just thinking out loud. Why, do you want to?"

Did she? "Sure. Yes. I've never done that before."

"Okay. So, what are you wearing?"

Devi looked down at her regular clothes. "I'm supposed to say something sexy, like nothing but an apron, right? But then you'd know I was lying. And it wouldn't be very sexy."

"Yeah, I would, and you're right, with anyone else it wouldn't turn me on. But hell, Devi, now you've got me thinking of you wearing nothing but an apron. How am I supposed to get through my day?"

She laughed and leaned her hip against the stove. His day? She wanted to forget work and curl up on a couch while they bantered back and forth like this. Which was odd for her. She'd never been much of a telephone chatterer, even in the early days of her past relationships.

"Listen, I'm sorry we had to leave early. Marcus and I had to go home and change before we hit work."

Devi traced her fingertip along the counter. "Don't worry

about it. I figured as much."

"I would have set your alarm, but I didn't know what time you went to work."

"Ten thirty. That's when we start prepping for lunch. I mean, for future reference."

"Okay. Good to know."

God, how little they knew about each other.

"I would have loved to wake up with you."

Tendrils of warmth crept around her. She snuck a guilty look around the empty room before she responded. "Me too."

"In that case, I'll wake you up tomorrow. I love morning sex."

"We had morning sex. That last time—"

Jace snorted. "Only in the strictest definition. I want to wake you up with my head between your thighs tomorrow."

"Sounds...promising."

His voice dropped an octave. "Then when you're nice and wet and panting, your tits jiggling, I'll fold back your legs and slide my cock deep inside you. Touch all those nice spots inside that you just love for me to hit. Slow and easy."

Whew. She didn't know what to say about that. Except, okay. Slow and easy worked just as well as hard and fast. "Are you thinking out loud again?"

"Are you turned on?"

Her nipples were drawn up tight. She could see them through her bra and T-shirt. "Yes."

"Then I think we're starting some phone sex here."

The door opening shot a jolt through her. She cleared her throat and turned her back as Asha pulled an apron off the hook. Instinctively, she crossed her arms over her all-too-obvious nipples. "Well, that's interesting, but I'm a bit busy right now. We can discuss this later tonight."

"What's there to discuss? You don't want me to work my dick inside that tight, wet—"

"That's not the issue right now. I just don't have time at the moment."

"I'm sorry. You can give me a blowjob first, if you like. You love that, when I fuck your face, don't you?"

Her face felt like it was on fire. "I'm sorry, I'm working."

He laughed. "Fine. Later?"

Yes please. Phone sex was all well and good as long as there weren't any witnesses. Well, except for Marcus and Jace. "Sure. Fine."

"Great. Oh, you guys close between two and five right?"

"Well, yes."

"Can you come out for a bit with us?"

Devi frowned. "Sure. Where?"

"Great. Marcus and I will pick you up at two."

"Um, okay. But where are we going?"

"See you then, baby."

The phone clicked on the other end and she folded it closed slowly. Why hadn't he answered her?

The clearing of a throat jerked her from her musings, and she turned to see Asha standing behind her. "There are a few orders already?" the woman asked in her softly accented voice.

"Yes. Yes, there are." The customers would be pissed, too, if they didn't get them soon. She turned back to the board, but the words swam in front of her like a mishmash of nouns. She grabbed two off the stack at random and handed them to Asha. "Here, you can get started on these."

The other cook gave her an odd look but hurried to the far end of the kitchen to prepare. Devi tried to refocus back on the food, thankful the orders were easy and mindless.

Perhaps Jace just wanted to get together for an afternoon quickie. Could a two p.m. quickie qualify as a nooner? She'd always wanted to try a nooner. She'd have to ask the men when they picked. Her. Up.

Shit.

Devi sighed. They'd need to rearrange their plans. No way could she let Rana catch a glimpse of her calmly getting into a car with the two men. In fact, she'd need to talk to them about staying away from the restaurant in general for the next couple of weeks. She couldn't just call and tell Jace that, though. Instinctually, she knew it would bother him. She'd have to tell them in person.

The orders came in steadily, and it was another hour before she could slip away to the restroom. She pulled out her phone and dialed Jace's number, only to be greeted by his recorded voice. Dammit. "He must have his phone off," she muttered. She checked, but he hadn't thought to input his office number.

Devi hesitated and then thumbed through her contacts until she came to Marcus's name. Both of his numbers had been programmed. She hated to call him at his office number. He could be busy. Then again, she hated to call his cell. He could be, well, busy.

Though she'd been just as physically intimate with him, she wasn't an idiot. Clearly, Marcus didn't want to be too involved.

She could text him. Devi perked up. Texts were suitably distant. She clicked on his name, and with the ease of a natural-born texter, tapped out a message. *Jace said u would pick me up at 2. Meet u 2 at library down street instead.* She hesitated and then continued, feeling bad for the subterfuge. *Have to return some books. Can u get a hold of him?*

There. If he didn't respond by one, then she would try actually calling him. She walked out the door as her phone buzzed. She pulled it out, unwilling to admit her anticipation.

*Fine.*

The anticipation fizzled. Devi's lips twisted into a wry smile.

Well, fine.

# Chapter Nine

Devi tapped her fingers against the railing of the stairs to the public library and squinted against the warm sunshine. She'd tried calling Jace again—about six times—but kept reaching his voice mail. Hopefully, Marcus had managed to head him off. Rana and Leena had both been hanging around when she'd left to make the brisk walk up one block.

A black pickup truck pulled into the driveway and cruised around until it parked in a spot right in front of her. Sunlight glared off the windshield, so she was unable to see the features of the big man until he stepped out of the cab, keys jingling in his hand. Devi blinked in surprise and spoke without thinking. "Are you sure you're an accountant?"

Marcus cocked his head. "Why?"

The huge pickup gleamed with chrome and metal. She sighed. "Never mind." Devi stopped looking at his sweet ride—did these men just trip over nice cars?—and studied the sedate black suit and subtle pinstriped tie he wore. She could recognize Jace's hand in the excellent cut and quality of the fabric. Marcus wouldn't care about such matters.

She realized they had fallen into an uneasy silence. She found it difficult to meet his eyes. For some reason, this was even worse than their first morning after. Would they have to go through this every morning?

"How are you doing?"

"Good." She felt like she should give him a hug, at the very least. She'd jump on Jace. With Marcus, though, she just wasn't sure of his reaction. She didn't want to presume.

He crossed his legs at his ankles and leaned against the hood of his car. The fine twill of his slacks molded against the muscles of his thighs. Did he work with a lot of women? A flash of jealousy shot through her system. He probably had to beat them off with a stick.

"You'd be doing a lot better if you were a little closer to me instead of way over there."

Devi raised a surprised gaze to meet his. His expression was enigmatic, but she glimpsed a wealth of watchfulness in his eyes.

*Why, he's as unsure as I am.* The knowledge gave her the courage to relax her tense shoulders and smile. "I could say the same for you. Why don't you mosey on over here?"

He crossed his arms over his impressive chest. "I asked first."

She snorted and mirrored his action. "You didn't ask. You made a statement."

"Babe, that's how I ask."

"Weird, *babe.* I ask with a raised intonation and a question mark at the end of the sentence. You should try it sometime."

The bark of laughter caught her off guard, and she started with surprise. She hadn't actually heard the man laugh once in their whirlwind weekend together. It sounded nice, better than nice, though a bit rough around the edges. Like him.

The slight smile remained on his lips, and he took a deliberate step forward, then another. And stopped.

Devi contemplated, for a split second, if she could make

him walk the rest of the way. If she held out long enough, he probably would. She had no real desire to see that fierce pride stripped bare, though. In all honesty, she was pretty impressed that he had at least made the effort. With little hesitation, she took her own two steps forward. Their toes touched, hers in her sensible low-heeled pumps, his in shiny wingtips. She looked up at him. "Hi."

Marcus's lips curved. "Hi." He leaned down. Devi expected a hard kiss of greeting, but instead he softly brushed his lips against hers. A big hand wrapped around her neck, and she twined her own fingers through his hair as he sipped at her lips.

Devi separated from him, breathless at the unexpected tenderness. She licked her lips. "You're right, I'm feeling a lot better."

He smiled, though his eyes were sober as he stared at her. She wanted to make him laugh, but she had the feeling she would need to slip under his guard again. "You got in touch with Jace, right?"

"Yeah." He nodded at the silver sedan that slipped into the parking lot. "There he is, actually."

The car glided up to them, and Jace rolled down his window and flashed her a grin. "Hey, beautiful. Need a ride?"

Devi smiled back. Some of the tension from her morning of worries melted away at the welcome and open appreciation in his eyes. "Sure, why not?" She ducked into the passenger seat Marcus held open for her and folded her fingers in her lap. "So where are we going?"

Jace leaned over and pressed a hard kiss against her mouth while Marcus clambered into the backseat. "Hello to you too. Did you get whatever you needed here?"

Devi was confused until she remembered her excuse for

meeting at the library. "Oh. Yes. Yes I did."

"Great." His coat was off, his shirt sleeves rolled up in deference to the midday heat. With easy skill, he drove out of the parking lot and down the street. "Hey, you're not wearing your new clothes today."

Devi looked down at her usual jeans and T-shirt. "I didn't have time this morning to pick out a new outfit." A partial truth. After so much upheaval, she had also just wanted her familiar clothes wrapped around her, no matter how much better the new stuff looked. Maybe tomorrow she would be brave enough to wear something different.

Jace played with her fingers. She liked it too much. To distract herself, she tossed a smile over her shoulder. "I have my new underwear on, though."

"Good," Marcus spoke. "I bought it more for us than you, so you're obligated to show us soon."

Devi laughed. "Good deal. So, why won't you guys tell me where we're going?"

Jace winked. "You'll find out when we get there."

"Why do I have the feeling I'm not going to like it?"

"Come on," Marcus said. "Have we done anything you don't like yet? Why would we take off from work to do something you won't like?"

"Are you okay with taking off from work? I know I keep odd hours. Will that be okay?"

"Don't worry about it. Marcus is high up enough on the food chain that he can claim a client meeting, and he had nothing else scheduled. As for me, I don't normally have anything on tap on Monday afternoons." Jace patted her on the knee in a reassuring manner, and then engaged her in light conversation about a ridiculous coworker, his hand heavy on her thigh. It wasn't until he withdrew to flip on his turn signal that Devi noted with some concern that they were in the slightly more rundown downtown area.

"Okay. So where are we going again?"

Jace's small smile did nothing to reassure her. They turned into an almost-deserted parking lot, pavement cracked, potholes aplenty. She stared with some confusion at the flamingo pink building all by its lonesome. No sign hung above the door. The bars on the windows certainly were not reassuring. "Is this... What is this?"

Marcus opened her door and she stepped out of the car. In an incongruously gallant manner that charmed her, he tucked her hand into the crook of his arm.

Jace led the way to the door, and he held it open to allow them entrance before him. The bell jangled merrily above her head. The interior was too dim after the bright sunshine, and Devi had to blink rapidly to adjust and see. Once her eyes adjusted, she blinked again, this time in surprise.

Why, it was a sex shop. Was that what people called it? Perhaps more of a novelty shop. Fun and sexy instead of seedy and skuzzy. The outside barely hinted at the size of the place. The floor space was impressive and arranged like an upscale boutique with strategic track lighting. Racks of lacy lingerie were interspaced with DVD spinners and bookshelves. Devi could see a vast array of—were those dildos?—along the back wall. Aisles containing even more risqué products were set up to the left and right.

"Surprise," Marcus whispered in her ear, and then kissed her neck.

She jolted out of her fascinated perusal and cast him a wide-eyed look. "I didn't know this place was even here."

"Come on, let's take a look around."

Devi resisted the pressure of Jace's hand at the small of her back. "Do we have to?"

Marcus linked his fingers through hers. "You promised, remember?"

She flushed, knowing they were all thinking of that session in the car. "Yes, but...can't we just do this online or something? I mean, what if we run into someone who knows us?"

"Then they'll be just as embarrassed as us, won't they?" Jace answered logically. "Besides, the owner is Marcus's client. I asked her when the slowest time of day was, and you can see the place is deserted. Come on."

Devi was touched Jace had been so considerate as to check that out first, but then she processed the rest of his words. "Her?"

Marcus smiled. "Miss Kitty. Of Miss Kitty's House of Pleasure. You've probably heard her more discreet ads on some of the local radio stations. Her yearly income is ridiculous."

Miss Kitty. What, was this a Wild West whorehouse? Devi pursed her lips, alarmed to find herself more than a little jealous of the sex-shop proprietor, who apparently knew her men well enough for them to give her a ring when they wanted to do some private shopping. "It's easy to make money off of sex." Surely that sanctimonious tone did not come from her.

Jace grinned. "Kitty's a firecracker. She's probably around here somewhere."

"How...nice." Oooh, she'd get to meet a woman who was probably on intimate terms with everything in this store. And who knew her men.

Whore.

*Stop being a bitch. They are not your men.* Devi took a deep breath.

"Are those my two favorite boys?"

Devi blinked. Instead of the low, sexy voice she expected, the words were whispery thin and quavery. A woman stepped around a rack of clothes and Devi wanted to laugh at her ridiculous misconceptions. The tiny woman must have been in her late seventies, at least, but she moved with a spring in her step and a twinkle in her bright blue eyes. She walked over to them and wasted no time in hugging Jace and Marcus. To her surprise, Marcus's hug was more heartfelt than she would have thought he possessed for a mere client, his face as soft as she had ever seen it as he gazed at the old woman. "How are you doing, Miss Kitty?"

"Oh, fine, just fine." Kitty clutched a bright red shopping basket in her dimpled hands and beamed at Devi. "And who is this pretty little lady?"

Jace swept a hand down her back. "This is Devi. Devi, I'd like to introduce you to Kitty. She saved our lives after she became one of Marcus's clients."

Charmed, Devi smiled and shook the other woman's hand. "Saved your lives?"

"With sugar cookies," Marcus said earnestly. "I'd forgotten what homemade sugar cookies tasted like."

"Don't forget the chocolate chip," Jace added.

"Don't let them fool you. Marcus saved my business when he pointed out that someone was embezzling from me. Fired my no-good son and hired my sweet son-in-law."

"None of my other clients thank me in baked goods, Miss Kitty." Marcus winked.

Kitty snickered. "The two of them are like bottomless pits. I hope you can cook, otherwise you're going to be eating out a lot."

"Devi's actually a chef," Jace said, with more pride than Devi expected.

Kitty's eyes widened. "Why, how interesting. You and I must exchange some recipes sometime." She cast a sly look at Marcus. "Though not right now. I assume you've been brought here for another reason, yes?"

Heat fired through Devi's cheeks. While speaking with the sweet woman, she'd forgotten she was surrounded by sex toys. "Umm…"

"Now, do you have a particular kink or a specific prop you're looking to cater to?"

*I am not talking to this grandmother about my kinks.* Devi took an involuntary step back from the helpfully expectant woman, but Jace halted her. "You know, Kitty, I think Devi might be more comfortable if we look around on our own first. We'll holler if we need anything."

"You do that, sweetheart. I just need to inventory the new batch of crotchless panties." With that announcement, Kitty shoved her basket into Jace's hands, patted Marcus's cheek with a wizened hand, beamed at Devi and walked toward the back of the store.

Devi stared after her and spoke in a hushed tone. "That woman is older than my grandmother. And I'm pretty certain my grandmother doesn't know what crotchless panties are."

Jace grasped her hand and began to lead her to the aisles lining the far right of the store. "She really is like our honorary grandma. I got grilled on the phone about you. I think she likes you."

"Wait a minute. So she knows? That you two…you know."

"Yes, she knows we, 'you know'," Marcus responded dryly. "The woman peddles sex. Not too much goes past her. And just think, now she knows that you, 'you know'."

Jace scowled at his brother. "Stop trying to embarrass her."

Devi sighed. "Well, at least she's not your real grandmother."

"Don't worry, we don't have any living grandparents. Or parents, for that matter."

Devi looked at Marcus in surprise. She hadn't even asked about their families, though with the sense of loneliness that radiated off them, she wasn't surprised they were alone. "You're orphans?"

Marcus's brows met. "Orphans are little red-haired girls. Our parents are dead. It happened a long time ago, it's no big deal."

"No big deal? My dad died when I was fifteen, but it still hurts."

"I didn't know about your dad, Devi. I'm sorry to hear that. Our mom and dad passed away when we were thirteen." Jace slipped an arm around her waist, drew her close and pressed a kiss against her forehead.

She leaned against his chest. "That's terrible, that you lost them both at once—"

"Hey, are we here for fun or for a grief-counseling session?" Marcus interrupted loudly. "'Cause otherwise, I need to get back to work."

Jace's arm tightened around her and she looked up in time to see irritation darken his face as he stared at his brother. He met her gaze and forced a smile. "Sorry. We can talk about this later."

Marcus snorted. "You two can talk, Dr. Phil." He grabbed her arm and pulled her away from Jace. "Come on. Let's have some fun."

Bringing Devi to a porn shop was more enjoyable than Marcus could have imagined. Jace and he didn't use a ton of props with their women, but those they did, they bought, as Devi had suggested, online. Not because they were embarrassed of Kitty's reaction to purchases in her store. God knew, a more sexually matter-of-fact woman than the geriatric probably did not exist. Marcus had never seen the point in making a special trip for the odd vibrator or anal plug for their fly-by-night women.

This, though, this was an experience. After an hour had passed, they'd barely walked down two aisles, since Devi seemed to be fascinated by every item they passed. Marcus didn't claim a working knowledge of every sexual prop ever made, but between him and Jace, they managed to explain some of the more complicated items. All three of them had become aroused after ten minutes.

"Nipple stimulators."

Her dark head jerked around, a curl brushing her plump cheek. "What?"

"These." He reached past her to pick up the box she had been studying, with two pink jelly structures pictured on the outside. Marcus pointed to the cups. "You place these over your nipples. See these nubs inside the suction cups? They'll tickle your nipples. You hit this little button, and they vibrate. Then, when you're about to go insane, you can squeeze these bulbs here and it'll feel like someone's sucking on you."

Devi licked her lips. "That sounds promising. I want those."

Marcus dropped them into the basket in his hand and grinned wickedly. "We'll use them, but you're pretty lucky since you have both of us. You know one of us will always want to play with these sweet little tits. Nothing can compare to the real deal, right?" He scraped a fingernail over her nipple, erect through her bra and T-shirt.

She inhaled roughly and shot him a mock glare. "Marcus, please. We are not in the privacy of, say, a dressing room here."

His blood fired up even more, both at her sassiness and the reminder of her "punishment" the day before. God, he just wanted to drag her out to the car...

Jace caught his eye at that moment and gave a subtle shake of his head. Marcus knew him well enough to know that was a "not yet." Jace had some sort of culmination in mind here, and it probably involved driving Devi's arousal even higher. Marcus wasn't about to screw that up. The woman was a wildcat when she was fully excited. He wanted some of that.

"Look, Devi, vibrators. Every woman needs one of those." Jace led her ahead of him down the aisle.

Marcus could see her roll her eyes. "Guys, I'm not completely ignorant. I have a vibrator."

Jace raised his eyebrows. "Yeah? Which one?"

"Um, I don't know."

"The Tiger? The Pearl? The Rabbit?"

"Vibrators don't have designer names. It's not like it's a Gucci purse."

Jace sighed, humor twinkling in his eyes. "Everything has designer names."

"It's purple, and it vibrates, and it makes me happy. That's all I care about."

Marcus caught up to them. "How big is it?"

Devi held up her hands a couple of inches apart.

Both men stared at the tiny space she indicated, and then each other, aghast. Marcus spoke first. "Honey, if that makes you happy, we must send you to heaven."

She started to laugh. Marcus loved making her laugh. *Don't think that.* It wasn't personal. She just had a nice laugh. Any man would like to hear it. *Yeah, right.*

"It's not the size that matters."

Jace smirked. "Yeah, okay." He picked up a package off the shelf and handed it to her. "Since you have a straight-up vibrator, you should try a dual action. The little head here will rub against your clitoris. You'll love it."

Her brow furrowed and she stared at the picture. "Okay. But it looks complicated."

Marcus slid his hand over her rounded ass. "We'll help you figure it out."

She cast him a look simmering with heat, and he almost whimpered as his cock engorged more. How was he supposed to wait?

"Well, I guess if you're going to help..." She dropped the box into his basket.

"This too." Jace handed her another box. "It's a clitoral stimulator." He moved closer, and Devi's eyes fell to half mast. Marcus knew she could feel the heat rising from each of their bodies, and that it turned her on. He stroked one finger down the curve of her neck and reveled in the slight tremor that coursed through her body. She was so receptive. Was it just them? Or would she be as receptive to any other man?

Anger accompanied that thought. He didn't want to think about Devi with other men, despite the fact he knew she wouldn't be alone for long once their little affair was over. The woman was too sexual and loving. Some other man, maybe even men, would benefit from all of the secret desires they were helping to bring to the surface.

No. He couldn't think of that. Marcus spoke to distract himself. "Do you know how this works?"

Devi looked at the box. "It...looks simple."

"It's like a G-string, but the vibrator fits right against your little clit. The remote has a twelve-foot range. So we can turn it on whenever we want you to go crazy." As Marcus spoke, Jace slid an arm around her waist, rested the palm of his free hand over the fly of her jeans and pressed gently. By the sound of her gasp, Marcus knew Jace had found her clit.

"Would you like that?" Jace whispered. "You could wear it under your clothes. No one would even know. When you're working, or reading, or grocery shopping. You'll never know when we'll turn it on. And in between, that hard little box is going to remind you who controls your pleasure."

Marcus could feel the shudder that ran through her body. "Sounds great. Let's go, guys."

Jace smiled enigmatically and withdrew his hand. "But we haven't even bought what we came for." He led her to the back of the store.

Along the way, Marcus grabbed whatever caught his eye on the shelves they passed and tossed the packages into his basket. He'd never been much of a toy man, happy to please his partner the natural way, but he wanted to try everything with Devi. She responded with such a complete lack of artifice. That shocked look of pleasure on her face? He wanted to keep it there, permanently.

Marcus caught up to Jace and Devi standing in front of a wide array of anal plugs. The anticipation on her face had been replaced by caution as she stared at the largest model on the wall. "Guys, I'm not sure if I really want to do this."

Jace kissed her neck. "That one is not for you."

"Well, the other ones don't look much more reassuring."

"You promised, remember?"

Devi let loose a disgruntled sigh. "I am not promising anything more when we are having sex. Got it?"

Marcus shrugged. "Well, don't tell us that, tell yourself. You're really easy." He pulled an array of plugs off the wall in different sizes and piled them in the now-overflowing basket. He turned to find Devi staring at the basket in dismay.

"If I don't like it, I'm using my safe word."

Marcus squinted. "Right. Since I haven't heard it yet while we were fucking you every which way, I forgot what that was. Refresh my memory?"

The corners of her mouth turned down. "Red, Marcus. The safe word is red."

"What a smart girl you are, Devi, to choose such an easy word."

Marcus grinned into Devi's horrified gaze as Kitty bustled up behind her. She chattered as she relieved Marcus of his basket. "You know, once I used the word 'cucumber' and my dear, late Harold, he completely forgot. I don't know why he thought I was screaming the word cucumber during sex. We were trying out a new set of restraints, and they were quite painful. So after that, I completely believe you should stick with simple words. Red is perfect, and I'm sure Marcus was just kidding about forgetting, right, Marcus?"

Marcus continued to smile. "Yes, ma'am."

"Are you three finding everything okay?" The woman poked through their basket and beamed at them. "Oh, are you new to anal pleasure, Devi?"

Devi squeaked.

"These will work well for you, but, Marcus, get that inflatable plug as well. I've heard that some women respond better to it."

Jace slipped an arm around Devi's waist. He was trying very hard to keep the smile off his face. "Thanks for your help, Miss Kitty. I think we're ready to check out."

"Wonderful! While you were shopping, I put a plate of cookies together for you. I just baked them yesterday." She cast a sly glance at Devi. "Though perhaps you don't need my cookies anymore."

"Oh no." Devi found her voice as they followed the little old woman through the store to the front checkout. "I'm not much of a baker, really."

Marcus thought back to the cookies he had filched from Devi's daisy-shaped cookie jar the night before. Either the woman was being modest or she didn't want Kitty to feel out of place. He guessed it was the latter, which touched him. Over the past couple of years, Kitty's fretting and fussing had kind of grown on him.

The speculative looks she was casting Devi as she rung them up were worrisome, though. Kitty'd been nagging them for months now that they needed to settle down. He didn't want the older woman to get any ideas. He would explain the nature of their affair to her later on.

Kitty finished filling three bulging, discreet paper bags full of their purchases, and then scurried around the register and gave Devi a hug, much to all of their surprise. She released her with a bright grin. "Boys, bring this sweet girl back again. It's been a while since I've seen a blush like hers."

Devi smiled and they all exchanged their goodbyes. As they walked to the door, Kitty called behind them, "And let me know how everything works out."

"I will kill either of you if you let her or anyone else know how anything works out," Devi said between teeth clenched in a smile, as she tossed a wave over her shoulder.

"We don't kiss and tell. You should know that much by now." Jace popped the trunk and they dropped their purchases inside.

Jace slammed the trunk closed and turned to face her. He extended a box to her. She took it from his hand and frowned at the clitoral stimulator. "What's this?"

"You have to go back to work."

Devi glanced at her watch. "I still have an hour. I thought we were going to go give some of these toys a test run..."

Jace tsked. "Now that's not nearly enough time, Dev, you know that. So here's what we're going to do." He nodded to the box in her hands. "I want you to go back to work and put that little toy on. But I'm going to keep the remote with me."

Without being told, Marcus stepped up right behind her, making sure she would feel his arousal pressed flush against her bottom. Over her shoulder, he could see right down the V-neck of her shirt. Her breasts rose and fell.

"I don't see how that's any fun for any of us."

Jace slipped his hands around her waist from the front and moved closer. "Because when we come in for dinner tonight I'll have that remote with me. And you won't know when, but that little stimulator is going to start vibrating, and you'll have to keep working." He brushed his lips against hers. "Would you like that?"

Marcus watched her long lashes flutter closed. "Yes. Wait. No." She opened her eyes and cast Jace a worried glance. "No. I almost forgot. You can't come to the restaurant."

Jace paused. "Tonight?"

"No. I mean, you can't come tonight, but I think it would be better if the two of you stayed away from the place while we're...together." She waved her hand in a vague gesture, as if to encompass their togetherness.

Had he not been so attuned to his twin, Marcus would have missed the fine tremor of disappointment and uncertainty that rushed through Jace. As for him, he didn't feel too much. He held no illusions about anyone, so nobody could ever really disappoint him.

That didn't mean, though, he couldn't get pissed on his brother's behalf. He tightened his hands around Devi's waist and spun her to face him. "What's the matter, sweetheart?" he crooned.

She blinked up at him, a startled doe.

"Marcus," Jace rapped sharply.

"Are we good enough to fuck, but not be seen with in public?"

Her eyes widened and then narrowed. "Do not take that tone with me. Did you or did you not want a girl who wouldn't get all attached? I seem to recall having a huge discussion about this in my kitchen yesterday. Remember, you railed against white picket fences?"

"Devi, it's fine." Jace's tone was soothing, but the glare he pinned Marcus with was anything but.

She shot him one last angry look before she turned to Jace. Marcus watched with resignation as his brother's glare was replaced with soft tenderness. Damn it. Devi may not see it, but Jace was so far gone over her it physically hurt Marcus. He didn't want his brother heartbroken.

Then again, it was early yet, Marcus consoled himself. The best way to cure Jace of this infatuation would be to let it play its course. They'd only been together for a couple of days, lust was still fogging all of their brains. Give it another week, no doubt Jace would be bitching about Devi's irritating quirks and faults.

*Oh yeah. All of those faults. Which would be...?*

Well, maybe the lust was fogging his brain too. She had to have faults. She was as human as anyone else.

"It's not that I don't want you to come," Devi interrupted his contemplation. "Rana will see you. And she will seriously freak out if she sees us so clearly together and go running to our other sister Leena." Devi shuddered. "You haven't met her yet. Leena's scary."

"Devi, so they find out we're still seeing each other. What could they possibly do?" Jace asked in a reasonable tone.

"Make my life miserable. You don't know my sisters. They'll drive me crazy." She wrinkled her nose. Marcus had noticed the little quirk last night. Could it be classified as irritating? No, damn it.

"So tell them to mind their own business. They're what? A few years older than you? Even if they were your parents, you're a grown woman. You can see and fuck whomever you want." Marcus's irritation surfaced in the gruff command.

Devi turned to look at him. "Our relationship is complicated." Her tone was chilly. Looked like he was still on probation for his jerkiness. "Even if I told them to back off, I doubt they would. They think I'm twelve and an imbecile when it comes to men." Her soft mouth tightened. "They'll come rushing in to save me from myself. It won't be the first time. I'd really rather just avoid it, if you don't mind."

Jace clearly minded, but he dipped his head in acquiescence. "We'll stay away from the restaurant for now."

Marcus narrowed his eyes. His brother was a whiz at verbal gymnastics. However, since Devi hadn't seemed to notice that tacked on "for now", he wouldn't call attention to it either.

She seemed satisfied, and Jace turned her attention when he tapped the box in her hands. "You still have to wear that.

Throughout work." He paused. "Why don't we meet at our place tonight?"

Marcus started. They never brought women to their condo. He opened his mouth, and then closed it again. He couldn't make a big deal out of this without making it seem like a big deal, and Jace knew that.

To her credit, Devi looked just as startled as he was. "Okay. I'll need directions."

Jace opened the passenger door for her. She slid in, the box clutched in her lap. "I'll tell you while I drive you back. When you come over tonight, we'll be waiting for you. In the meantime, I want you to feel that little weight brushing against your clit as you walk, talk, cook. I want you to pretend it's my finger."

Her skin flushed. "Sounds good."

Marcus caught the door before Jace could close it. "One thing. No matter how crazy it makes you, you're not to come. If you do, we'll know. And we will punish you. Got it?"

The apprehension and lust in her face drove him crazy. "Got it."

# Chapter Ten

Why had she ever agreed to this nonsense?

It didn't even matter that the clitoral stimulator wasn't vibrating. The tiny box attached to the thong-like underwear nestled perfectly against the taut button of her sex, stimulating her regardless.

Too damn honest, that was her problem. She should have just slipped the little device on when she was on her way home, and she wouldn't have had to suffer through hours of unrequited desire while she cooked up delicacies for the unusually heavy Monday evening crowd. Then again, she couldn't lie worth a damn. Next time she might actually deliberately disobey them, since she kind of wanted to see what her punishment entailed, but tonight she wanted to play with more of these intriguing toys they had purchased.

She walked to the hook on the wall to hang up her apron and shuddered at the resulting sensations. Her panties were soaked.

"Hey, Dev, you on your way home?"

Devi jumped at Rana's voice and turned to where she stood in the doorway of the darkened kitchen. "Yes. I was just closing up here. My turn." Every night, Leena handled the money, Rana was responsible for the main floor and Devi closed down the kitchen. The three of them switched off on general close up.

"Okay. I'm renting a movie. Want to come over and watch with me?"

"Uh, no, that's okay. I'm so tired." Devi faked a yawn and felt foolish.

It seemed to work, though, since Rana didn't question her. "Rain check, then. Do you need a ride home?"

"I brought my car tonight."

"Wow, that's not like you."

Devi shrugged. "Didn't feel like walking." A partial truth. Jace and Marcus's home was too far to walk.

Even if she was going to her house, she didn't think she'd be using her feet in the next couple of weeks. Forget the fact that work was only a couple of blocks away from her home along brightly lit streets that bustled with activity, even at ten p.m. Jace had freaked out when she'd admitted she regularly walked to and from the restaurant. Not so different from her sisters, actually, each of whom looked for excuses to drive her home at night.

Unlike her sisters, Jace and Marcus had a wonderfully gifted way with words, and after an intense lecture on the car ride from the porn shop, with images of her potentially raped, mutilated and desecrated body dancing in her head, she'd finally conceded and promised to use her car in the evenings. *Sorry, environment.*

It seemed like a simple thing to give in on, and if they had her wearing more toys like the one nestled against the heart of her sex, she wouldn't want to walk for any prolonged period of time. As it was, she'd be jumping her men for the remote as soon as she got home. If just the slight pressure and weight of the stimulator could make her this crazy, imagine the fun she could have when it started vibrating.

"I'll see you tomorrow then." Rana paused at the door.

"You're sure you're okay, right?"

"Rana, I am begging you, please don't ask me that all week."

Her sister's smile was sheepish. "Sorry. I promise, I'll let it drop. And I have to say, you definitely have a spring in your step today. I'm so happy to see it."

Devi kept her smile in place until Rana left. Thank God she didn't know the source of that spring.

She rushed through the rest of the procedures to close down the restaurant, unable to spare more than a minute of the time necessary to do so. By the time she set the alarm and locked the door, a fine tremor of anticipation had her hands shaking.

Devi turned the key in the ignition of her cute little Nissan and pulled out the piece of paper in her pocket on which she'd scribbled Jace's directions. She felt rather conflicted about going to their place. Somehow it made the relationship seem more legitimate. Protocol probably dictated they meet in a hotel room or something, but she had a frugal soul. Why pay fifty bucks for a shady bed when she had a free one?

Luckily, the upscale address wasn't too far away. Within ten minutes she pulled into the driveway of a two-story white condo with a dual-car garage. Her headlights slashed across the front of the small home. Neither of the twins' cars sat outside, and the windows were dark.

She killed the engine and got out of the car slowly, comparing the number on the address in her hand to the one above the garage. They matched, but she didn't want to knock on the wrong door at this hour of the night. Devi slipped her cell phone out of her pocket and pressed the number to speed dial Jace.

He picked up on the first ring. "You're late. Where are you?"

She smiled at the uncharacteristic impatience in his voice, which matched her own. “I think I’m outside your house, but your cars aren’t outside, and I wanted to make sure before I knocked.” As she stared at the front of the house, a curtain moved in one of the upstairs windows.

“I see you. I’m just hopping in the shower, I’ll be right down. Come on in.”

She hesitated and then opened the unlocked door. Despite all they’d done together, it seemed far too intimate to walk inside their home without knocking.

“Nice,” she muttered as she entered the condo. The condo was cookie-cutter perfect and boasted that new-home smell unique to modern constructions. A dim bankers lamp lit the high-ceiling foyer. A hardwood staircase spiraled up to the second floor, and a balcony overlooked the foyer. Spotless white tiles lay in a diagonal pattern on the floor. Since she always did at home, and fearful of marring the tiles, she slipped her pumps off and grimaced at the coldness of the ceramic under her feet. Tile throughout might be the rage in most Florida homes, but she loved her shag carpeting and plush rugs. Who wanted to walk on cold tile?

“Make yourself at home,” Jace yelled down, and she jumped. She could hear the water in the shower starting, and for a second she considered joining him and scratching the itch they had stoked for her.

Hmm, have shower sex or poke around their house?

Since she didn’t see or hear Marcus anywhere, the latter idea was too tempting to turn her back on. Giving in to her curiosity, she wandered into the dark dining room. Sleek, ultramodern black and white furnishings decorated the place. A black dining table had been set with placemats and china and looked like it had never so much as been touched. She couldn’t imagine the delicate plates in front of Jace or Marcus. Framed black and white abstract paintings hung on the white walls. She shivered. The décor left her cold, not a touch of personality or individuality to lighten the place.

She escaped into the adjoining kitchen, where someone had left the under-the-cabinet lighting on. She sighed a bit over that convenience, and allowed her hand to coast over the black granite countertop with only a hint of covetousness. On the whole though, the kitchen was far too small to do any kind of serious cooking.

Despite the shortcomings of the room, Devi couldn't resist giving one last pat to the stainless-steel double fridge before she walked through the other opening of the kitchen. She felt for the light switch on the wall and found it. A smile touched her lips.

Because, clearly, this was where her men spent most of their time. Instead of cold designer furniture, a battered leather sectional and chair took up most of the space, centered around a huge flat-screen TV. A fleece blanket lay crumpled on the foot of the sofa, magazines were spread open on the surface of the coffee table. A basketball had been left beside a pair of large sneakers kicked off in front of the recliner. The walls were bare of anything but the large TV, though, and unlike her own home, there were no pictures of family and friends to clutter up the surfaces.

No, wait. She walked to the entertainment center flanking the TV and picked up one of the two gold-framed photos. A family portrait of four, so sweet and picture-perfect she couldn't help but smile at the attractive dark-haired couple. The woman and man beamed with pride while they each held a bundled infant in their arms. *Their parents.*

She put down the photo, feeling vaguely intrusive, and

picked up the other frame. This one was of Marcus and Jace. Judging by their casual jeans and the sweatshirts emblazoned with their university name, she pinned their ages to about their college years. They each had longer hair then, their faces unlined, their expressions far more somber and serious than she would have expected on men so young. She'd gone to culinary school instead of college, but she'd certainly been far more carefree than these two.

Their personalities were evident in the photo. Jace's body was angled toward his brother, as if to protect him. He gazed at the camera with steady regard. Marcus, on the other hand, looked cynical and tough even then—his lips curved in a subtle sneer, his eyes narrowed and distrustful.

Devi swept her finger over his face. What had happened in his life to make him so gruff and cynical at such a young age? Had it been the loss of his parents?

*No, no, no. No! No psychoanalyzing. Danger, Will Robinson.*

She placed the photo on the shelf and backed away, though she realized her alarm was vaguely ridiculous. However, she was not going to stand here pondering the mysteries of these men. That train of thought did lead to danger, absolutely. Short-term sexual partners did not worry over each other's psychological states.

"I didn't hear you knock."

She spun around, her hand pressed against her chest. "Oh. Marcus. You startled me."

"I was in the garage."

He stood in the kitchen doorway in only a pair of unsnapped jeans. A sexy smear of grease highlighted his rock-hard abs. Involuntarily, her gaze slid over his bare chest, the arrow of hair that trailed into his open jeans. She was suddenly all too aware of the little toy she wore, forgotten while she'd toured the house.

"Um, Jace told me to just come on in. He's upstairs, showering. I hope that's okay." He didn't say anything. "I like your house. Or what I've seen of it."

"Take off your clothes."

She blinked. "Wow, you're not one for social niceties, are you?"

"Are you hungry?"

"Not really."

"Do you want a drink?"

Devi slicked her tongue over her lips. "No. I'm good."

"Good. Take off your clothes."

"Marcus." She frowned, though she really wanted to laugh.

"I want to see if you're wearing the stimulator."

"I said I would, and I am."

"You wore it from the minute we dropped you off?"

"Yes."

"I don't believe you."

Devi stared at him, confused. "What?"

He grinned and slid his hand into his pocket. The first gentle vibration had her legs stiffening in shock. The little box came alive, rubbing against her already-stiffened clit like the finger Jace had likened it to. She relaxed and allowed the slow pleasure to sink into her bones. Marcus didn't allow her time to appreciate it, and he must have turned a dial up somewhere, because the vibrations against her over-stimulated clit increased in their intensity. She moaned and leaned against the couch, her legs boneless and incapable of supporting her weight.

A low male chuckle reached her. "I think we can believe

her."

She opened her eyes to find Jace standing in the room as well. Clad only in a sexy pair of black boxer briefs, water still glistening on his chest and hair, he watched her with a small smile and narrowed eyes already heated with lust.

Just as her climax yawned before her, the soundless stimulation ended. "What are you doing? Turn that back on, this instant."

Marcus tsked and walked forward until he stood right in front of her. "Didn't we discuss you giving us orders?"

Heat rose from his body. All of the relentless unappeased desire from the day welled up inside of her. She frowned at him. "I was about to come."

"We don't want you to, yet."

"I don't care," she said waspishly. "Turn that damn thing on again or one of you fuck me here." Amazing how a couple of days of ceaseless pleasure could lower her inhibitions—she felt no hesitation in making the demand.

"No." With that simple announcement, Marcus startled Devi by scooping her off her feet.

She shrieked and grabbed on to his shoulders. No one had carried her since she'd been a small child. Pudginess had crept up on her at a young age, so even her father had declined picking her up. "I'm too heavy for you. Put me down."

He ignored her and spoke to his brother. "Where are the supplies?"

*Supplies?*

Jace studied her with predatory interest. If she hadn't already been soaked, that look would have done it. "In my room."

"Did you hear me? I'm too fat to be carried around like

this."

Marcus walked out of the room and back into the grand entryway. He glanced over his shoulder. "I think the toys were a bad idea. They've made her way too contrary." He jostled her until she tightened her arms around his neck in reaction.

"Stop talking about me like I'm not here. Wreck your back, see if I care. And the toy doesn't make me contrary. Hours of sexual deprivation make me contrary."

"Then you should be nicer to the men who are going to end that deprivation," Marcus explained patiently. "In the meantime, why don't you pretend your hero is carrying you off to be properly ravished instead of worrying about your damned weight?"

Devi paused. He had a point. Once she thought past her sexual frustration, of course. She relaxed into his arms. "Sorry. I'm not a very good heroine, I guess."

He handled the dark stairs with ease, not even breathless. He turned right at the top of the stairs and entered a tidy bedroom lit by soft track lighting. Peripherally, she got the impression of heavy wooden furnishings and a huge four-poster bed. Marcus looked down at her, his face cast in shadows. "That's okay. I'm no hero."

She slid her palm over his jaw, the slight stubble catching on her skin. "I think you're doing a pretty good job."

Devi caught the hardening of Marcus's jaw under her hand. "Then your judgment sucks." With that harsh pronouncement, he dropped her on her feet. She stumbled back. The backs of her knees hit the mattress behind her, and she sat down.

Since they were both underdressed to begin with, it didn't take more than a minute for Marcus to kick off his jeans and Jace to skim his boxer briefs down his legs. After viewing them in the buff so many times now, Devi could make out differences in their physiques that were easier to overlook when they were decent. Jace was an inch or two shorter, his muscles lean while Marcus was bulkier.

In the package department, the twins had been blessed with equally beautiful penises. Man, when she got lucky, she really hit the jackpot. For a second, Devi was overwhelmed with the knowledge that she didn't just get one of these excellent specimens, she got two.

*On loan.*

Yeah, yeah, whatever.

"Like what you see?" Jace's tone was amused and indulgent.

Devi managed to tear her gaze away from his huge member and smiled teasingly. "Always."

"Take off. Your. Clothes." Marcus's hands clenched and unclenched at his side.

She responded to the heat in his gaze and stood up from the bed with a seductive little shimmy. Her shirt and bra she tossed in the same direction as their clothes. Their eyes tracked over the swell of her full breasts, and she tossed her hair. She had damn good boobs.

When her fingers stroked down to the snap of her jeans, though, she hesitated. *Cellulite. Love handles. Dimples.* Her bottom and thighs were not her friends.

Marcus must have mistaken her hesitation for a tease. "All your clothes."

Devi shot a quick glance to the overhead track lighting, even less forgiving than her bedroom lamp. "I don't guess you'd consider turning off the light this time?"

"Nope."

She sighed. "You two are the contrary ones. If I said I

wanted the lights on, you'd snap them off in a heartbeat."

Jace grinned. "Too bad you didn't think of that before, huh?"

Marcus shot her a disbelieving look. "We've seen you naked already, did you forget?"

She squirmed, the air-conditioning cool against her tightened nipples. "I don't like my butt, that's all. It's not attractive."

Jace squinted at her and wrapped his hand around his bobbing cock. "Do you think we get this hard for unattractive asses?"

"Are you serious? I don't understand women at all. I like your butt. In fact, I love your butt," Marcus replied emphatically. "If you take your jeans off, I'll show you how much I love it. I'll love it so much, you won't be able to walk in the morning."

She gulped and unsnapped the top button. "Let's not get too hasty, here."

Marcus walked over until he stood right in front of her. He brushed her hands aside and took over the chore of unzipping the pants. He slid his hands inside the loosened waistband and pushed the jeans down. She wore only the G-string/stimulator. "Too late. You've challenged me. I'll have you loving your ass as much as I do by the end of the night."

Apprehension and anticipation danced along Devi's nerve endings, drowning out the twinge of self-consciousness. As her clothes pooled around her feet, Marcus tightened his hands on her waist, picked her up with little effort and tossed her back on the bed. She bounced once and then settled into the giving mattress.

Marcus crawled up her body like a hungry cat, the muscles in his biceps and chest flexing. She twined her arms around his neck and drew his head down to partake of his passionate kiss.

"So sweet," he breathed against her lips. He tilted her head to the side and licked down her neck. His hand shifted and the vibrations started again. His hard cock pressed against the swatch of material that hid the little box of the stimulator, and she moved against him, frantic to get off.

He groaned and slid his big hand under her ass, lifting her hips up. She rode against the thick ridge, her legs spreading wider, her head tilting back against the pillows. She was so close, she just needed a little more...

"Please. Please let me come."

"I love it when you beg," Marcus murmured.

The vibrations increased in intensity, and Marcus thrust his hips against her in a rhythmic motion, mimicking sex. If the panty hadn't been there, he would be inside her. One hard push of his cock opened the folds of her labia so the stimulator came in perfect contact with her clit. She screamed and fell apart, her empty cunt grasping at nothing while her release passed through her.

The shudders of pleasure were still racking her body when Marcus turned her over so she faced the side of the bed. He positioned her on the bed as if she were a rag doll, arranging her on her hands and knees. The stimulator had been shut off, thank God. Her clit felt a little oversensitive. "What are you doing?"

The question was answered when Jace stepped into her direct line of sight, his hard cock at perfect level with her mouth. Without being told, she reached out with one hand, the other supporting herself, and stroked the hard flesh, using his own lubrication leaking from the tip to make the surface slick and shiny.

He sank his fingers into her hair and urged her forward.

She teased him by flicking her tongue over the head. His sharp inhalation preceded the thrust of his hips, which lodged the tip of his cock inside her mouth.

"God, your mouth. Your mouth was made for fucking," Jace moaned. She glanced up his body to find him watching her. His high cheekbones were ruddy with color, his eyes narrowed in intense concentration. Devi rubbed her tongue along the underside of his sensitive cockhead, and his thighs tensed.

She loved this. Loved the feeling of feminine power. She controlled their pleasure, made these big strong men slaves to her mouth and body.

"Her whole body was made for fucking." Marcus's hands closed over the globes of her bottom. "Especially this ass. I'm going to fuck this ass." He squeezed both cheeks and separated them.

Devi's eyes opened wide in alarm and flew up to meet Jace's gaze. He shook his head. "Not tonight. We need to get you ready." He must have felt the tension in her body, because Jace used his grip on her hair to pull her off his cock. It popped free of her mouth, the plum tip red and gleaming with her saliva. "If you really don't want it, say the word."

A minute ticked by while Devi considered her options. All the while, Marcus kept up a steady kneading of her ass cheeks. They wouldn't continue if she told them to stop. This was all about new experiences, though, wasn't it? If she really hated it, she could have them stop later. She shook her head.

Jace wasn't satisfied. "Tell us you don't want us to stop."

"Don't stop. Unless," she amended, "I tell you to. I don't like pain."

A sharp slap resounded in the room as Marcus tapped her ass with his palm. Renewed moisture coated the lips of her pussy and she shuddered. The bed squeaked as he moved away from her, and then she heard the rustle of a wrapper. "Some kinds of pain are good."

She couldn't argue with that. Mostly because Jace had begun feeding her his cock again. He was considerate, giving her only little restrained thrusts so she didn't take too much.

Too considerate, since she wanted more. She wanted him as wild and out of control as he made her. To that end, she bobbed her head deeper on him, until the head of his cock hit the back of her throat. She held him there and swallowed, as they had taught her. The rough groan Jace gave rewarded her.

As did his large hands, which tightened around her head. She welcomed the slight sting of pain as her strands caught in his fingers. Devi doubled her efforts, and her obvious willingness to please him spurred him past his own control, his hips thrusting against her mouth with no consideration to her gentler sensibilities.

"Yeah, baby. Take me deeper."

The bed depressed behind her, and Devi jumped when two large hands spread the cheeks of her ass wide.

Oh God, were they going to start right off the bat with one of the plugs? Which one? Even the smallest seemed horribly large to her as she imagined the variety they had bought. Her entire body tensed.

"Is she being a bad girl, Jace?"

His hips stopped thrusting, and Jace cradled her head, his thumbs pressing in to her cheeks so the soft lining of her mouth caressed his hard cock. "She's certainly not paying enough attention to me."

Could it be possible for a man to whine when his penis was in a woman's mouth? Devi frowned up at him as best as she could to convey her irritation, his erection resting against her tongue. Saliva pooled in her mouth and she swallowed, inadvertently sucking him in deeper. He grinned and stroked her hair. “Stop getting so nervous. If you hate it, we’ll stop, okay?”

Their gazes held. She didn’t know why she trusted these men so much, but she did. They had only been interested in her pleasure until now. That wouldn’t suddenly change tonight. She nodded.

“Good girl.” Jace gave an imperceptible nod, and the little vibrator in the thong she still wore turned on. She jumped with the unanticipated sensation. Marcus brushed the fabric aside and Devi felt the jelly-like substance of a foreign object, though not where she expected it.

Marcus placed the vibrator against the entrance to her pussy, and the nubby plastic scraped her inner walls as it entered. She groaned around her mouthful of cock, and Jace shuddered above her before he withdrew, his cock wet and practically vibrating with need. Her lips were bruised, her body empty despite the plastic phallus inside her. It wasn’t enough. She wanted her men inside her, everywhere.

“Please, someone just fuck me.”

Instead of complying, Marcus fucked her with the toy until her arms and legs could barely support her.

Just when she thought she would go mad, Jace stood and walked around behind her, giving her an unimpeded view of the large dresser mirror. Despite her need, she had the presence of mind to be shocked by her appearance on all fours, her breasts hanging full and heavy below her. Her face was flushed red and looked different, the lips fuller, the eyes wider. She met Jace’s gaze in the mirror.

“You’re beautiful,” he murmured.

She felt beautiful.

"Raise up your ass, Devi," Marcus ordered, and without thought, she complied, her ass arching up to his hands. In the mirror, she watched his face as he left the vibrator inside of her and stroked a reverent hand over the curve of her bottom. His face was intense, his expression worshipful. He looked up to find her watching him, and his face hardened. He slid his thumbs under the straps of her thong and worked it down. Though the thin strip of material hadn't provided any real protection, she shivered at even that lack of covering.

Jace removed a tube from the dresser and squirted a generous amount of the lube into his palm. He handed the tube to Marcus, who squirted some onto two of his fingers and surprised her by sliding them inside of her.

Devi inhaled sharply, the coolness of the gel a marked contrast to the heat of her flesh. Marcus stretched his fingers inside of her for a too-brief moment before he withdrew. In the mirror, Jace laid both of his slick hands on the curve of her bottom, and she tensed. Jace squeezed the muscles of her ass and shifted position. In his new stance, he blocked her sight of Marcus's hand, deliberate, she was sure. "Relax. I told you we wouldn't be fucking your ass tonight. Trust us."

Jace rubbed her bottom and then moved up her back, finding the tense knots she didn't even know she possessed and manipulating them. "Close your eyes."

She did not comply, and he reached underneath her to give her nipples a quick, sharp tweak. She gasped, as the flesh was already super sensitive. "Close your eyes before I blindfold you."

His tone was mild, but Devi had no doubt he would carry through on the threat. She slid her eyes closed, and all of a sudden she could only feel. The cool air washed over the crack of her ass as one of them separated the cheeks, and the other turned the vibrator in her pussy on. The shock made her jump and then moan in rising lust. A hand on her back forced her upper body lower to the mattress, and the cotton rubbed against her sensitive nipples.

One of the men began to thrust the vibrator deeper into her body. Just when she thought she would scream with frustration, the slick, round head of the plug entered just an inch or so inside of her anus. The foreign sensation had her eyes popping open in shock as her pussy spasmed on the slick plastic of the vibrator. Oh, that was good. It hurt, yes, a little bit, but rather like the spanking did, in a good way, and it drove her pleasure even higher. She rocked back against Marcus and he chuckled.

"You like that?"

"Yes, oh yes. Please, more."

Obliging, for once, he slid the plug in a little at a time, until the flared base lodged against the opening. Weak from the shudders of confused pleasure coursing through her, she took the sensations as the vibrator was lazily thrust in and out. Her pussy walls clenched around it and she worked her way to a huge orgasm.

Until, of course, the dildo was pulled free from her protesting cunt. "Please, I'm dying here."

"I can't wait to fuck this ass," Marcus growled.

"Just think, Devi," Jace spoke up, his finger following the line of her spine. "That plug is way smaller than our cocks. Imagine how good it's going to feel. Ten times better than this."

Ten times? She would die. She let out a little whimper of submission.

Marcus cupped his hand over the base of the plug in a protective gesture. "Soon, baby. But right now...right now I want you to get a little taste of how it's going to be."

He angled his penis lower and used the tip to separate the lips of her wet sex. Jace's hands coasted up her back as Marcus began a steady pressure.

Devi's eyes flew open in shock. With the plug lodged in her ass, she felt completely invaded by Marcus's thick cock. He felt a hundred times larger than ever before.

"God, you're so tight," he groaned in agonized pleasure, and lifted her unresisting body up, arranging her legs outside of his and pressing her back to his front. His hands grasped her knees and spread her legs wide. The folds of her cunt opened, her clitoris exposed, a fact Jace took immediate advantage of.

She screamed at the first touch of his rough fingers against the little nubbin, particularly since it came just as Marcus clenched his fingers around her hips and started to thrust, short, strong digs of his penis. Jace kept his finger still, while she and Marcus took care of the movement. With his other hand, Jace fondled her breast. When she whimpered in pleasure, his head dipped down, and he pulled the nipple into his mouth, drawing in strong tugs.

The plug in her ass, the cock in her pussy, four hands roving over her skin, lips finding all of her sensitive spots... The pleasure was too much to bear, and within a few minutes she came, shaking between their arms.

Through the pleasure, she felt Marcus freeze and groan as the walls of her cunt clenched again and again on the thick intruder inside of her. The condom muted the heat of his release.

She collapsed back against him, sweat gluing her back to his chest. "I'm done," she whispered, and closed her eyes.

They popped open again when strong hands pinched her nipples. "I think you've forgotten something." Jace pulled her off of Marcus and arranged her on her back, her legs draped over the side of the bed.

"I'm tired."

He leaned down and kissed her. His penis brushed against the saturated folds of her cunt. "How is this fair to me?"

She yawned loudly. "Can I just give you a blowjob?"

Jace laughed. "No."

Devi spread her arms out and opened her legs. "Fine."

"So gracious." He kissed her again. "I'll try not to bother you too much."

Without any preliminaries, he put his hands under her knees, spread her wide and rammed into her. She gasped, her too-tired body immediately responding to the new pounding. Nerve endings flared to life. Devi hadn't thought it possible, but her second release was even more intense than the first.

Jace shouted and arched his back as he came. The expression on his face was so beautifully intense, she could have watched him forever. The dreamy haze of satiation followed the focused concentration of his lust, and he collapsed on top of her, his body a heavy weight.

# Chapter Eleven

Nothing could make him move. Devi had wrung him dry.

Jace nuzzled her sweaty neck. Even her sweat smelled good to him, a combination of cinnamon and spices.

"I brought you food."

Her muffled announcement from beneath him had his stomach sighing in happiness. Damn, but the woman was perfect.

"You didn't have to do that." He lifted himself up and off to the side to give her a bit of breathing space, though he missed her stroking fingers.

"Yes, she did. I had a frozen dinner hours ago." Marcus put down the glass of water in his hand. He stood by the bed, wearing a pair of boxers. He must have freshened up while Devi had been busy slaughtering him.

"I forgot it in the car. There's a cooler in the backseat. Everything should be fine."

"I'll go get it. You two can get cleaned up."

Jace sighed silently. Marcus never had any interest in pampering the women they were with after the sex was finished. He hoped that changed. Nothing was more intimate than caring for a woman they had just shared.

He disengaged from Devi's boneless arms and turned her

over, despite her murmur of protest. They had used the smallest-sized anal plug, but she still whimpered when he removed it from her body. He shuddered with renewed lust when he remembered how she had taken the plug. It had been so hot. He couldn't wait to slide his cock into that tight little hole. Or watch Marcus do the same while he penetrated her pussy.

He rubbed her generous ass in comfort, squeezing the flesh in his hands. He loved that she was so soft all over, more than a handful. No hard angles or bones, just warmth and plush flesh.

Jace scooped her up in his arms and smiled when she nuzzled against his chest. Clearly, she was too tired to protest being carried.

In the interest of time, since he knew Marcus would be returning, Jace turned on the shower instead of drawing a bath. She stood there yawning under the spray of water while he dealt with his condom and nestled against him when he got in behind her.

His heart clenched a little bit at the way she leaned against him, so trusting and sweet as he washed the soap off her and then dried her. He was just patting her down with the fluffy towel when he heard Marcus enter the room again. Jace brushed a kiss against her forehead and lifted her again, towel and all, to go back to the bedroom. God, he was so far gone over her. He'd barely been able to control his impatience while he'd been waiting for her to come to their house.

Devi's request that they stay away from the restaurant had disappointed him, but after he'd thought about it, it made sense. He needed to control himself and have faith that she would fall just as fast for them as he already had for her. Jace consoled himself with the thought that the restriction was only temporary.

In the meantime, he could enjoy the sight of her in his bed. He wasn't too attached to their house, and actually preferred the warmth and comfort of her own home, but there was something singularly satisfying about seeing her surrounded by their possessions. They'd never brought another woman into their domain, and that thought was pleasurable enough.

"Did you heat up everything?" Devi asked.

"Everything but the stuff in this insulated pack." Marcus held up a black bag.

"Good, that's dessert. It's best at room temp."

Jace watched as she sank into a lotus position on the bed, the towel tucked around her tightly, held with a knot between her breasts. He wanted to rip the towel off.

Before he could do just that, Marcus finished spreading out the plastic take-out containers on the bed and reached out to tug at the terrycloth. She held on to it for a second. "Aren't we going to eat?"

Marcus tugged again and shrugged. "What does eating have to do with you covering yourself up? Everything should be done with you naked."

Devi didn't bother to protest much more, probably because she knew it wouldn't be effective. The towel slipped away. Her shoulders hunched forward and her hand made a restless motion, probably seeking to cover herself.

Since Jace knew the action would spur Marcus, and hey, he wanted to eat, he leaned across the bed and dipped his head to take one nipple and then the other one into his mouth. When her body relaxed, he pulled away to examine the tight, wet, brown points. He smiled into her eyes, trying to convey the admiration and appreciation he felt for her body in his eyes. "Beautiful," he murmured.

The flush in her skin remained high, but Jace noticed she

straightened her shoulders a little bit and allowed her full breasts to remain on display. She'd come quite a way in just a couple of days.

Marcus had already dived into one of the containers and Jace opened the one closest to him, finding rice. He picked up the plastic spork and dug in to it, pleased to find a layer of cashews, chicken and vegetables on the bottom. "This is good," he said with his mouth full.

She smiled and leaned against the headboard, seemingly accustomed to their nudity. "*Biryani.* I know your favorite dish, but we ran low on mutton and I wasn't sure what else you guys liked, so I just brought a little of everything."

"Perfect." Marcus put down his dish and opened a new container, sampling the contents, what looked like steamed dumplings. "We like everything. Next time, bring a lot of everything."

Jace took another bite of the rice dish, savoring the burst of spice and flavor on his tongue. Once when he'd been particularly hungry last week, he'd dripped ketchup on instant rice and inhaled it. Devi was going to seriously spoil him. He noticed she hadn't touched anything. "Aren't you going to eat?"

She eyed the dumpling Marcus was eating with relish and then shook her head, with reluctance, it seemed. "I eat too much while I cook. You know, the sampling and all. So I try to skip having a big dinner. Otherwise I'd be as big as a house."

Jace frowned. He hated to think she was depriving herself. "Are you hungry?"

She shrugged. "I'm okay."

Marcus scooped up another dumpling with his fingers and held it out to her. "Think of this as sampling."

With good nature, Devi gave in and leaned forward to eat the dumpling. Jace watched Marcus closely, unable to miss the narrowing of his brother's eyes as Devi ate the food he offered from his fingers. The intimacy of the act must have registered with Marcus, because as soon as she was done, he dropped his hand and focused on demolishing the dish.

Well, Rome hadn't been built in a day. These were huge strides for Marcus. Jace took over where his twin had left off, teasing and sneaking a bite here and there into Devi's mouth, until she laughed and held him off, claiming a full stomach. He could feel Marcus's mood turning somber while he watched them interact. Jace hated it, but there was nothing he could do. He couldn't change Marcus's entire mindset for him.

Jace had long finished his own food and was kissing the side of Devi's neck when Marcus cleared his throat and stood. "Well, that was great. Thanks, Devi."

Devi looked up with surprise. "You didn't have any dessert." She reached for the insulated pack and withdrew a plastic Tupperware container.

"I'm not really hungry for dessert."

Jace snorted. "You're always ready for dessert. If you haven't noticed, he has a sweet tooth like you wouldn't believe."

"Really? I'll keep that in mind."

"Don't put yourself to any trouble for me." Marcus's reply was brusque, and Jace could have kicked him.

The teasing smile in Devi's eyes faded, her shoulders hunching a little. Her fingers moved in a little restless movement and Jace knew she was seeking a cover to hide behind again. Her reply, though, was calm and controlled. "Whatever you want."

Marcus looked between the two of them. "Yeah. Well, I have to get to bed. Early day and all that."

Devi's entire body turned rigid. "No one is stopping you.

Good night."

Marcus hesitated for a second before he nodded once and stepped back. "Right. Good night." He didn't meet either of their eyes as he left the room.

Jace sat up and cleaned up the empty plates, stacking them on the nightstand. He'd take them down later. "It's not you, you know," he said in a low tone, unable to meet her eyes. If he looked into those liquid eyes, he'd never be able to keep the ugly truth from her. It would spew out. Marcus would never forgive him. "He doesn't sleep with anyone."

"I don't care," she said. Jace knew she was lying. A woman like her wouldn't stand for being fucked and then kicked out of bed. That was precisely why he'd always been careful to make sure that the women he and his brother enjoyed in the past were as cynical and tough as they were, to minimize any emotional damage.

He wouldn't call her on it, though—he understood pride. "Okay," he said softly, and wrapped his arm around her. Her shoulders stayed rigid for a second, and he rubbed his hand up and down her arm.

"Do you want me to leave?"

"No." His response was swift and sure, and it must have reassured her, because she relaxed against him. He hugged her closer. Leave? She'd be terrified if he admitted he wanted her to stay in his bed forever. Normal men did not fall in love at first sight like this, did they?

"You know, my sweet tooth isn't quite as well developed, but I have a healthy fondness for dessert," he teased, trying to turn her attention. She smiled and sat up to open the container before she handed it to him.

He studied what appeared to be little balls in syrup. They looked dubious, but Devi hadn't yet served him anything but amazing food. He picked up the plastic fork. "What's this called?"

"*Gulab Jaman.* It's really just fried dough in syrup."

Jace cut into a ball, scooped up some of the syrup and took a bite. The sweet perfectly balanced the spicy aftertaste from the other food. Delicious. He looked into Devi's expectant little face and fixed a serious expression. "It's not nearly sweet enough."

Her brow furrowed at the criticism. "What?"

Jace speared the rest of the ball on his fork and shifted his body, turning toward her. In the process, he oh-so-clumsily dribbled some of the syrup on her breasts. She shrieked and then laughed when he tipped the container, upending the entire dish on her body. The little fried balls rolled over her body, one landing perfectly in the curls of her pussy.

"Your bed is going to be ruined."

"I'll buy a new one tomorrow." He licked the sweet sugar off her tits. "Now this. This is sweet," he murmured, and proceeded to lick and eat every bit of sugar off her.

When he sank into the tight depths of her body, her cunt still clenching from the orgasm he'd brought her to with his tongue, all he could think was that he'd found heaven.

How fucked up was he, though, that he couldn't enjoy it without a part of his brain wishing he could share this slice of peace with his brother?

# Chapter Twelve

"Devi, are you even listening to me?"

"Huh?" Devi looked up to find her second oldest sister, Leena, frowning at her from across her desk.

"I said, you aren't paying attention. Are you okay?"

Devi glanced down at the paper in front of her as if it would hold the answer to whatever Leena had been discussing. They usually met early every Friday evening to plan the following week's menu. Since Leena rarely had much time during the rest of the week, Devi enjoyed their one-on-ones together.

But today she just wanted to put her head down and take a nap. She hadn't slept in a week. As soon as work ended after ten, she raced home to find her men waiting. And who wanted to sleep once they touched her? She felt a burning need to make the most of every hour they had together, since they couldn't really see each other during the day. Jace and Marcus were able to rearrange their appointments, but they still had to report in to work in the mornings, and Devi cooked during the lunch and dinner shifts, which pretty much eliminated the time when most normal people scheduled dates.

"I'm so sorry, Leena. I guess my mind's just not in it."

Leena rested her arms on the clutter-free desktop and linked her hands together. A slight frown wrinkled her brow. She squinted behind her fashionable dark-framed glasses.

"Your mind hasn't been on anything lately. Do you want to talk about it?"

Devi restrained the urge to squirm as if she faced the principal instead of a sister three years older than her. Leena and Rana were barely ten months apart, and the two of them couldn't resist joining forces to play mother hen. In turn, she found it more difficult to hide things from them than she did from their mother.

She could just imagine the drama if she really spilled the beans. "Well, you see, Rana set me up with this pair of brothers who are really into threesomes. She thought it would loosen me up a bit. Boy howdy, did it! In fact, it loosened me up so much I agreed to have a two-week-long affair with them. I haven't been sleeping because we fuck like rabbits all night long, and I'm upset now, because I just realized I'm falling in love with two men, and how is that possible? By the way, have you ever tried an inflatable butt plug? They're awesome."

Devi shuddered, picturing Leena's head exploding, messing up her ruthlessly straightened hair and soiling the perfectly tailored power suit clinging to her athletic body. That would be before she castrated and killed Jace and Marcus. And maybe Rana, too, if she got in the way. Oh, and that porn shop where they had bought all those lovely toys? Burnt to a crisp. 'Cause her baby sister shouldn't know anything about sex.

So instead, she said the expected thing. "Nope. Nothing's wrong. You know, just one of those weeks." She started to gather up her papers. "Are we finished? This menu looks good to me. You can put the specials page to print."

Leena narrowed her eyes and sat back in her swivel chair. "Okay. So..." She turned this way and that. "Are you bringing anyone to the party tomorrow?"

Oh God, the party. She had almost forgotten Leena's

thirtieth birthday bash. Devi felt a pang she couldn't bring Jace and Marcus. She'd love to see them interacting with her friends and family. There was no way she could do that, though. Both her sisters, her mother and various family and friends would be there. Maybe she could just introduce them as friends? Except then she'd have to watch assorted females try to cozy up to them. No, she'd just tell them she had a family thing and try to sneak back to her house as quick as she could. "Nope. No one."

"You're not seeing anyone?"

"Um, no."

"Huh." Leena stared at her hard before glancing away. "I could have sworn... So what's with the new clothes?"

Devi glanced down at her new jeans and cobalt blue T-shirt. After their explosive encounter at the twin's condo, she'd started out the next day by wearing one of her new outfits, and continued every day afterward. They were in effect the same clothes she always wore, but Jace had done an excellent job paying attention to cut, quality and color. Her new clothes fit her so much better and flattered her body instead of concealing it. Her confidence had built with every compliment and assessing glance she'd received in the past week. "It was just time for a change."

"But no man?"

Devi didn't speak.

"Hmmm...okay. Well, anyway, I was thinking, Mama told me Auntie Preiti has her cousin's nephew's son from India visiting." Leena's tone was carefully casual. "Would you like me to invite him to the party?"

Devi blinked. "Are you turning into a matrimonial website now?"

"Of course not. It's just that, well, he sounds really nice, and he's a doctor..."

"And he needs a green card?" she asked dryly.

Leena cast her a chiding glance. "Like that's the only reason someone would want you?"

"No." Jace and Marcus had taught her differently. "Why the sudden interest in my love life?" Were both of her sisters chatting with cupid lately?

"See, Mama, me and Rana were talking about it a couple of weeks ago, and we're worried. You haven't dated anyone since Tarek." She spit the name out as if it had a bad taste. "And we just want you to be happy. You're not still hung up on him, are you?"

"Hell no. I got over him the minute our relationship ended." That explained Rana's motivation to introduce Devi to a ménage experience. Clearly Rana had interpreted the Big Three summit findings to mean Devi needed some sex in her life in order to demolish any lingering feelings for Tarek. Rana's misplaced guilt over her part in the way Devi's last relationship ended probably urged her to find the most pleasurable, fantasy-inducing, one-night stand she could. Devi spared a moment of warmth for her oldest sister. Thank God she had introduced her to Jace and Marcus.

"...he's just obtained a work visa, and you know how that works, it won't be long before he's here for good."

Devi sighed. Meanwhile, it looked like her mother and Leena thought the best cure for her imaginary broken heart was to see her wed and bed. "You can invite him if you want, but I'm really not interested. Maybe Rana would like him?"

"Rana would chew him up and spit him out. Devi, it's just that you're so well suited for marriage and babies and forever."

She had become angry when Marcus had said the same thing not even a week ago, but now she didn't have it in her to protest. It was true. She liked being a part of a couple. Or at least, the right couple. Was there such a thing as being part of a few?

She stood from her chair. "I'm fine, okay? Besides, don't you know the youngest daughter isn't supposed to get married first?" she teased. "Everyone will think you and Rana are old maids."

Leena rolled her eyes. "I think we both know Rana has no intention of settling down."

"What about you?" Devi asked curiously. "I mean you and Rahul have been together for like three years now."

Leena laughed, but avoided eye contact. Not for the first time, Devi wondered if her sister wasn't as happy in her relationship as she pretended to be. No great loss—Devi didn't care much for Rahul, anyway. "Don't you worry about me." She shuffled some papers onto her already-clean desk. "By the way, I saw your note. You need next Thursday through Saturday off?"

"Um, yes, if that's okay. I just need a couple of days for myself," she added, before Leena could ask why.

Leena shrugged. "Yeah, that's fine. I was going to tell you to take some time off anyway."

"Great. So, I'd better get back to the kitchen. I guess you're heading home soon?" Friday was Leena's one official night off. Devi and Rana had practically had to browbeat her to accept even that much time to herself, but they were more than able to handle the busy night without her. Since Leena, as manager and a certified workaholic, was often inside the restaurant before either of them even woke up, it was only fair.

"Oh. Yeah, in just a bit."

"Okay. See you tomorrow." Devi closed the door behind her and leaned against the wall, breathing a sigh of relief.

The dinner hour would be starting soon, so she would need to be front and center in a few. Then just a couple more hours and she'd get to go home.

Home. Devi resisted the urge to do a quick jig. Despite her lack of sleep and the strain of the necessary subterfuge from her family and friends, she had never been happier.

The past few nights had flown by in a haze of sexual excess and personal discoveries. The sex was amazing, but Devi found the moments in between equally precious. Perhaps it was the sense of urgency around the whole thing, but she felt as though she knew more about them than she had ever learned about her previous boyfriends after months of dating. The more she discovered, the more she slapped her forehead for her stupid big talk of an affair with an expiration date.

Jace was easy, gentle and romantic. Easy to like, and easier to love. He soaked up any sign of affection and reciprocated it in a way that made her feel cherished and adored as never before.

Marcus was a tougher nut, but his rough edges called out to the dormant caregiver in her. His smiles were few and far between, so she often felt as though the sun had come out when she was able to tease one out of him. Twice she had even been able to coax a belly laugh out of him, and the look of surprise on his own face had squeezed a vise of tenderness around her heart. His affection was more gruff, but all the more intense for his reluctance to display it.

They had taught her so much about herself. She had never considered herself a sexual person, but she must have hit some prime she hadn't realized, because she'd turned into a certified nympho. Perhaps it also had something to do with them, though. Never had she felt confident about her body. She had no problem parading around her house butt naked in the morning with sunshine streaming all around her. She saw herself through their eyes and felt like Miss Universe. For once in her life, she wasn't someone's baby sister or daughter or a good cook, she was a woman. And yeah, she might still get a bit of an ego trip that two such attractive men found her pretty, but now she was a bit more, well, proud that these particular men found her special, not just to have sex with, but to talk and laugh and eat with every free moment that they had. Because they were special.

They should be special together.

*Argh.*

She straightened, slapped the papers she held against her thigh and shook off the melancholy that had settled over her. She knew what she had been getting into. Marcus had made it very clear what he thought of a happily ever after. Just because she suddenly found herself with a ridiculous urge to enter into a real relationship with two men after only a week of knowing them didn't make it a remotely plausible outcome. That sort of thing didn't happen in the real world. She needed to get over it before she ruined what little time they had left.

She walked into the main dining room on her way to the kitchen and stopped dead, certain she had conjured up the man from her thoughts. Because there sat Jace at his usual table, perusing a menu. She looked around frantically, but didn't see Rana. Had luck smiled on her? Was her sister on break or off messing around with someone else's love life? In that case, she needed to get Jace out now before one of them gave away something they shouldn't.

Without even being conscious of it, she flew to his table. "What are you doing here?" she whispered in a furious undertone.

With irritating calm, he put the menu down, looked up and

smiled at her. “Hey, honey. I got done with work early, so I thought I would just pop on over and grab a bite here.”

She clenched the back of the chair opposite him. “Didn’t we discuss this?”

“Me, eating?”

“*No.*”

“Getting done with work early?”

“Marcus is right, you are irritating.”

The teasing in his manner vanished when she blinked at the sudden sting of tears. “I wanted to see you. Is that a crime? I’m not going to strip you naked here.” He injected just enough hurt in his voice to make her feel like a royal bitch.

“No, of course it’s not a crime. I’m just—I’m trying to make this as easy as I can.” She must have sounded as bewildered as she felt, since he reached out to grab her hand and brought it to his lips, his gaze soft.

“All right, babe, you’re right. I’ve kind of had a rough day, and I needed to see you.” He gave her a halfhearted smile. “Just looking at you makes me feel better.”

Her heart fluttered at that announcement, while her common sense sounded its alarms. People in affairs should not be seeking out their partners for comfort outside of the bedroom. Her common sense had always been a pushover though, and she heard herself ask, “What happened today?”

“It’s kind of a long story.” He rubbed her fingers between his. “You know that couple I was telling you about?”

Devi knew Jace handled more than his share of pro bono cases, much to his colleagues’ collective dismay. Devi didn’t think he would even consider turning someone in need away. He spoke of his clients as a whole with respect and compassion, and was definitely involved in their problems and lives.

As he detailed the setback the couple had endured that afternoon in court, she slipped into the seat next to him and watched the play of emotions on his face whilc she held his hands in silence.

He finished the story and they sat for a minute before he roused himself. "I'm sorry, I'm keeping you from work. I'll get going..."

"No." The fine thread of tension in his body had diminished, but she didn't want him driving when he was still upset. She could deal with Rana. She hoped. "It's fine, stay. I'll take my dinner with you, 'kay?"

"Are you sure?"

"Sure."

Jace squeezed her fingers and leaned in to place a kiss on her lips. "Thanks," he said hoarsely.

"Ahem."

Devi looked up to find Leena standing next to the table, and suddenly became aware of the intimacy of their pose, their hands clasped, heads together, his thighs bracketing hers. She drew back and stood, but from her sister's gimlet stare, knew it was too late.

Leena sized Jace up, and bless his heart, Jace returned the regard. She arched an eyebrow at him, and Devi knew he barely resisted doing the same. "Devi, I thought you said you weren't seeing anyone."

He glanced at her, and though his expression remained inscrutable, she thought she saw a flicker of...hurt? "Um, well, I..."

Jace turned back to her sister, stood and held out his hand. "Leena, right? I'm Jace Callahan. I think we've exchanged business cards at a couple of chamber meetings."

Devi held her breath. Rana had mentioned rumors abounded about the twins. Had Leena heard them? No, that didn't appear to be the case. Some of the suspicion eased from Leena's face as she shook his hand, no doubt approving of his firm grip. "I'm sorry, you meet so many people there. What company are you with?"

"Gunther-Searcy. We had a couple of lunches catered from here before I started coming here regularly. You've done a great job marketing this place."

The name of the prestigious law firm might as well have been a key to Ali Baba's cave, as far as Leena was concerned. She looked him up and down again, and Devi knew that by the time Leena had gone from his expensive haircut to his designer shoes, her sister had probably nailed his net worth down to the penny.

Leena admired ambition. And snazzy dressers.

She smiled warmly at him and cast a teasing glance at Devi. "I'm sorry, you know what a private person Devi is. Why, none of us had any idea she was seeing anyone special."

"Yeah, Devi's private, all right."

Now why had he made it sound like a condemnation? "Don't you need to leave, Leena?"

"Hmm? Oh, yes, of course. It was great to meet you." She shot a narrowed look at Devi that promised prying at a later date, before turning back to him. "We'll be seeing you at the party tomorrow, won't we?"

"Jace is doing something tomorrow night," Devi blurted out, desperation rising.

Both of them ignored her. "No, I'm not. I'd love to be there. Your birthday, right?"

"Yup, the big 3-0. You'll get to meet our other sister. She's out right now, had to run an errand."

Well, at least she wouldn't have to deal with Rana tonight.

"That's great. Hey, we could make it a family affair," he added casually. "Do you mind if I bring my brother?"

The wheezing sound she made must have been low enough to bypass Leena's hearing, but Jace reached out to twine his fingers around hers.

"Not at all." Leena beamed at him. "We're very family oriented."

"Oh, me too," Jace said earnestly.

"Great, well, I'll see you then." With a nod at Devi, Leena took her leave with a bright smile.

No doubt General Leena had already started planning the wedding. She whirled on Jace as soon as Leena was out of earshot. "Are you crazy?"

"No, why?"

"Why?" Devi ran her hands through her hair, fisting handfuls of the strands, before lowering her voice to a furious whisper, conscious of the trickle of diners coming in to the restaurant. "Because Rana is going to be at that party tomorrow. Rana, who set us up to have a threesome, but has no idea we've continued this relationship. And I'm sure there are going to be other people there who know exactly what you and your brother are up to, and when they put the two of you together with me, rumors are going to fly."

He dropped his hand away from hers and regarded her with a cool look. "What did you want me to do? She caught me off guard."

Devi breathed. "Okay. Okay, we can make this work. Maybe you and I can just go together, make a quick appearance and leave." They didn't even have to appear to be a couple. The party would be large enough that they could just drift through it separately.

"What should I do, tell Marcus to sit at home?"

"Well, why not? It's not like Marcus is really the type of person to enjoy birthday cake and party hats, is he?"

Jace's jaw tightened. "Are you ashamed to be seen with us?"

Devi stared at him. "Are you kidding me?"

His face hardened, and for a minute he looked so much like Marcus Devi had to blink. "Sorry, I forgot we were just a fuck for you. Do you need us to service you tonight, your highness?"

"Keep your voice down." Was he actually hurt? "We all agreed to what this relationship would entail."

"No." He grabbed his suit jacket and slipped it on with jerky movements. "You and Marcus agreed. I knew what I wanted from the beginning and this wasn't it. I had thought I could change your minds, but clearly a couple of weeks of fucking isn't enough to form any kind of basis for a relationship."

She covered her mouth with her hand, watching him with blurry eyes. "Jace..."

"Save it. I don't want to hear anything." He nodded to her, his eyes black with anger and hurt. "See you later tonight. I assume our *agreement* is still in effect."

He didn't wait for a response, but stalked to the front door. Devi let him go with a helpless feeling. After he left, she roused herself enough to check for witnesses, but they must have conducted their conversation in such low voices, no one had noticed.

Devi speed-walked into the kitchen and grabbed her apron. She nodded to the others in the room and began scrubbing her hands. While her outer movements were unhurried and automatic, her brain clicked along at a terrifying rate.

Jace had not intended for this to be a quick fling for any of them. He had gone into this with the intention that they would continue to see each other indefinitely. Which meant he had stronger feelings for her than just lust or liking. She paused, her hands clenching on the damp towel. Could he be falling in love with her as she was with the two of them?

For a moment, she felt a terrifying guilt, that she had feelings for the two of them when Jace was focused only on her, but then she reminded herself that he clearly didn't mind having the three of them together. In fact, he insisted on it.

She considered that as she tossed some potatoes into the oven to bake. Had the two of them ever had relationships separate from one another? If not, had they ever had a relationship, period?

It could never work. Could it?

# Chapter Thirteen

"Stupid, stupid, *stupid*." Jace barely resisted the urge to bang his head against his steering wheel.

What devil had prompted him to go to the restaurant tonight? So he'd had a bad day. Did he have to go running to a woman to kiss his owie?

He had felt so much better once he had talked it over with Devi, though. She had that ability, to make him feel like he was a greater person than he really was, even when they were just silent together. She listened when he spoke and helped him put his problems in perspective.

When they were together, he believed he could be worthy of someone decent and good like her. She nearly brought him to tears because he knew she made his brother feel the same way. God knew Marcus needed someone to give him that feeling.

So, after he had purged himself of his bad day, he'd been riding high, high enough that he finagled an invite to a family party for him and his brother. For a second there, he completely forgot that they weren't a normal couple.

Of course Devi had been upset about any gossip that might come about. Despite Rana's outward brashness, he had the feeling Devi and her family were fairly conservative. She'd spoken of her sheltered childhood and teenage years. Her father died when she was young, but her mother and sisters kept strict watch over her, so she'd had a delayed introduction to dating and sex.

Devi and her sisters were thoroughly American, but clearly some cultural traditions were still followed in their household. Threesomes probably weren't what they wanted for their baby girl.

He breathed out a sigh. Why the hell hadn't he just kept his mouth shut? His original plan had been to slowly push forward the deadline of their affair, easing their way into her life, seducing every one of her senses until she had no choice but to keep seeing them, until she couldn't imagine a life without them.

If he'd stayed quiet, he could have enjoyed a nice dinner with Devi at the restaurant, and pretended in his own mind, at least, they were a normal couple.

Instead, he was sitting in his car four hours later, in the dark, parked outside her house like a desperate stalker.

*Stupid.*

He jumped a bit when the passenger door clicked open. The interior light flared on for a second, blinding him, before Devi slid inside and shut the door.

"Hey."

He leaned his head against the headrest and stared ahead of him. "Hey."

Silence. If she wanted him to leave, he would. Actually, if she had stalked into the house without even acknowledging him, he wouldn't have blamed her.

"I brought dinner."

He turned his head in surprise. Devi touched the top of the brown bag in her lap and Jace realized the scent of spice in the air wasn't Devi's alone. He brought himself to meet her gaze.

The moon shone through the window, creating luminous shadows in her eyes. She looked back at him steadily, no tears or anger or panic, only calm searching.

It took him a while to comprehend she was waiting for a response, so he gave a jerky nod. "Okay."

She opened the door and stepped out, and he followed suit, not quite sure if he was dreaming. Did she want to tell him to get out of her life over dinner? It seemed odd, to invite him in and then kick him out.

He walked behind her to the door in silence. She bent her head as she struggled to fit the correct key in her lock. Any other night he would have taken advantage of her position and softly kissed his way along the nape of her neck. For once, he couldn't predict what her reaction would be.

So he trailed after her as she made her way to the kitchen and unpacked the Styrofoam containers. She put the rice and chicken curry on a large plate with fluid movements. He leaned against the doorframe and watched her for a moment, and then found his customary forthrightness. "Do you want me to leave?"

She didn't look at him, but stuck the plate in the microwave and pressed some buttons. "Why would I have invited you in?"

He shrugged. She walked to the fridge and withdrew two bottles of his favorite brand of beer. Jace had been touched when she had noticed what he liked to drink, but now only felt miserable when he realized half a pack still sat on the top shelf. Devi didn't normally drink beer, so she'd probably just toss it.

She twisted off both tops and handed one to him, taking a healthy gulp of the other. She finally met his eyes. "Where's Marcus?"

"He has an HOA audit tonight. He'll be late."

Devi nodded. She'd already heard Marcus gripe about the

annual home owner's association audits that were required by law, and the fact that they could extend into the early hours of the morning if the boards weren't cooperative enough.

The silence stretched until Jace couldn't take it anymore. "Please forgive me."

"I'm sorry."

Jace blinked. They had spoken at once. "What?"

"What do you have to be sorry about? I'm the one who acted like a bitch."

To his horror, tears filled her eyes. Worry over his reception forgotten, he crossed the kitchen and gathered her in his arms, running a hand over the delicate length of her spine. "You're never a bitch. I'm sorry I pushed. It's not your fault that I had different expectations I never shared."

She sniffed into his shirt and rubbed her face back and forth, and, at that moment, he couldn't think of any better use for the two hundred dollar garment than as her handkerchief. "I do wish you would have said something."

"I didn't want to scare you. I knew I was asking a lot."

"It was never about just sex with you, was it?"

He shook his head, and then realized she couldn't see. "No."

"Why me?"

He paused. She didn't sound tortured, only confused. He chose his words with care. "Because the first time I saw you, I felt like I'd been run over by a truck. Like we were the only people in the room. I've never even had a physical connection like that to anyone. I would watch you smile and I felt like the sun was coming out. And now that I know you... Are you crying again?"

She buried her face deeper in his shirt. "You're so sweet.

Why didn't you just ask me out?"

With a shaky hand, he smoothed her hair down. Here it got twisted. "Because I didn't just want you for me. It's one thing to have sex with a woman by myself, but I can't have an emotional connection with a woman who doesn't feel the same way toward Marcus. I wanted you for both of us. I knew Marcus would feel the same way I felt, though he'd be hard to convince. I figured if you were meant for us, the sex would draw you in. And in the meantime, I could buy us some time to work on the rest of it."

She raised her head, her lashes wet with tears. "Congratulations. I have feelings for both of you. Do you have any idea how difficult such a relationship would be? Do you know how tough it would be for my family to accept this? I'm not a person who can hide things easily."

"I'm not asking you to."

Her tone was plaintive. "Why does it have to be both of you?"

He rested his forehead against hers and closed his eyes. "It's a long story. And it's not all mine to tell."

"I think I have the right."

If anyone did, it was her. How could he ask her for blind trust in something so unconventional and wacky without at least trying to explain their reasons? He nodded slowly and let go of her. He couldn't touch her right now, and he turned his back so he wouldn't have to see her. He crossed to the large picture window and looked out at the postage-stamp yard outside.

"Our parents died when we were thirteen. A freak car accident. Their tire blew, and they ran into a semi."

"My God. You didn't tell me how they died. That's terrible."

"Yeah. That would have been bad enough, but

unfortunately, they had also left us a pretty large estate." He laughed mirthlessly. "They were great parents, but not very forward-thinking. They hadn't bothered to appoint guardianship to anyone. So both sides of the family went to war." His tone softened. "Our father's brother, our uncle, is wonderful. He didn't care about the money, he was just devastated about my dad dying. We still talk to him. He did his best, but when it came right down to it, he didn't have the money our mom's family did. Her sister and her husband took us in." Even today, Jace couldn't bring himself to call them his aunt and uncle. He stopped, lost in his memories, until Devi's hand stroked along his back. He allowed it for a minute before he twisted away, unable to bear her touch while he told the rest.

"I'm smaller than Marcus."

"Not from my point of view."

A smile lightened his gloom a bit. "Not like that. Sometimes when a woman's carrying multiples, there's a dominant twin, one who's bigger or healthier. We were born premature, but Marcus was almost a pound larger. He was in the regular nursery, I was in the NICU in an incubator.

"Even now, I'm a bit shorter and leaner than him, though I worked out like a maniac in college to fill out to the size I'm at. You wouldn't have even realized we were identical when we were kids. I was a runt, scrawny and all legs and arms."

"I bet you were adorable."

"Maybe to my mother. Other kids loved to pick on me. Marcus fought more than one fight for me, and after a while, they left me alone. He was larger than most of the other kids by then.

"So when we were taken in by my mom's sister, Marcus was already used to fighting my battles. It didn't take us long to figure out our dear old uncle was a sadistic bastard and our aunt a cheap whore with the maternal instincts of a barracuda. They both told us we were worthless so many times I lost count. They dreamed up ways to punish us for the slightest infraction. Once I got my wrist broken because I left a wet towel on the floor. I'm pretty sure our uncle took up smoking just so he could put the things out on our arms and legs. There was nothing he loved more than whipping the snot out of us. No, that's not right. There were a couple of other things he loved more." His lips tightened, and he looked in the window, at the double reflection there. "Shall I keep going, or do you want to tell the rest?"

"You have no right."

Jace turned around and faced his brother, standing ashen-faced and trembling within the doorway. "She deserves to know."

"She doesn't need to know."

Jace kept his eyes locked on Marcus's. "When our uncle realized how protective Marcus was of me, he decided to use it against us. He told Marcus if he cooperated, he'd leave me alone until we were old enough to leave.

"We'd tried to tell people about the abuse, but the bastards were so good, everyone thought it was just grief over our parents talking. So, of course Marcus felt like he had no choice."

"Shut *up*."

"So he let the son of a bitch molest him."

Devi's soft cry of anguish rang out in the room, silent but for his measured words. "We never talked about it, because I couldn't protect him, so what was the point?" Jace's voice broke on the last word. "He did that, and I knew he did it for me, so the bastard wouldn't touch me.

"I knew it screwed him up. He didn't date anyone, didn't

even try for sex. Then during our senior year of college, I brought home this crazy girl who had a fantasy of doing it with twins. And for that little bit of time, it was like everything was back to normal."

"Asshole." The growl left Marcus's mouth a split second before he launched himself across the room. Jace took the first punch as his due, the split lip as his penance, but ducked for the second.

The anger that rose with the uppercut to his jaw had its grounds in years of frustration, in a fate that had been needlessly cruel to two little boys. With a roar of his own, he shoved his shoulder into his brother's chest, knocking them both toward the counter. He heard a distant crash and Devi's distressed cry, but nothing could stop the two of them from pounding their aggression out on each other.

They were well matched, had been almost the same size for some time now, and though Marcus still had bulkier muscles, Jace's lean frame allowed him to move faster. Jace managed to get a good shot at Marcus's right eye, which snapped his head around and had him teetering back. At the last second, Marcus snaked a leg through his and twisted so he landed on top of him.

Jace was bracing himself for a nasty blow when he felt a sharp stream of cold water hit his face.

"What the fuck?" Marcus reared back.

With water dripping across both of their faces, they turned toward Devi, who stood holding the extendable hose from the sink. She tightened her finger on the trigger in clear warning. "The next one to raise a hand in my kitchen is getting a bath."

~ ❁ ~

"Moron."

"Asswipe."

"You're both idiots," Devi snapped over Jace's and Marcus's mutters. She slapped a steak—a prime cut, intended for a nice dinner, damn it—over Marcus's eye and tried not to soften over his visible wince. She nurtured the irritation she felt over the two of them brawling in her kitchen as if it was a saloon in some back alley.

Because if she wasn't mad, she'd probably just sit down and cry.

She'd known there must be some sort of dark secret in their past—neither of them were forthcoming over their younger years, even though Jace had no trouble opening up about anything else in their lives.

She didn't pity them, since they were two strong men who wouldn't want her pity. She did ache for the young orphans they had been, abused by the people who should have protected them. She hurt to think of Marcus, so strong and arrogant, being at anyone's mercy, and Jace, so loving and protective, left helpless.

It explained a lot. Jace's machinations, Marcus's wariness and aggression. Even their sharing, which went way beyond a cheap sexual thrill into a necessity. They needed the connection the ménage brought to them. If Devi was a psychiatrist, she would probably have a field day with it.

She wasn't a psychiatrist, though, just a woman who cared deeply for both of them, already on the road to loving them.

Devi leaned against the counter and crossed her arms, studying the two of them as they sat sullen at her little breakfast table. "Have you two ever tried counseling?"

"Hell no."

Jace only snorted, though he was careful not to dislodge the pack of peas he held to his split lip. Another cut lay near his eye, and Devi was sure there were probably a few more bruises under his clothes. Marcus hadn't fared much better—his black eye was already swelling, and a blue shadow tinged his jaw. Devi had always thought seeing two men fight would be rather thrilling, but she could do without it when she wasn't quite sure which one to cheer for.

"I'm still not clear on why you needed to open your fat mouth," Marcus grumbled. "Why was today so special? We were doing okay without having a big share fest."

"Because I needed Devi to understand that she wasn't just some cheap ass for us, that the novelty wouldn't wear off and we'd walk away. I told Devi I plotted to have her fall in love with both of us," Jace admitted.

"I knew it. I knew all along you were crazy over her. What the hell were you thinking?"

"Fuck you. You could have left at any time. You wanted to be with her as much as I did, but I'm man enough to admit it."

Marcus slapped the steak on the table and glared at his brother. "Why don't we go outside and figure out who's more of a man."

"Stop it, this instant." Devi came to stand between them. "I have a hose outside too."

The two of them barely listened to her, their gazes locked on each other. "That's your problem," Jace sneered. "Always trying to settle things with your fists. It's not that easy. I want this. I want a semi-normal life. I want a woman to come home to, someone to share my life with."

"I never stopped you from having any of that."

"There is no way I can have any of it, unless I know you're getting it too. You think I haven't tried to go out with a woman by myself, to build a life separate from you? You think I don't know about those women you've taken to cheap hotel rooms somewhere so you can try to do the same thing?" Jace shook his head. "It's not possible for us. When I saw Devi, I fell head over heels for her, and I knew you would too. I prayed she'd be able to accept both of us, and I am not going to let your self-destructive tendencies screw this up for us."

"Oh, yeah, what woman wouldn't dream of being married to two men?"

Married? Devi's eyes widened. She hadn't really thought of it that way.

Jace made a frustrated noise. "Devi cares for us."

"Yeah, well, she also cares for her family and friends, and their good opinion of her, I'm sure. It's one thing to fuck two men, another to bring them home for Sunday dinner. What does she get out of it?"

"Two men who adore her, who appreciate her and the happiness she brings us."

"Two perverted men who were physically and sexually abused. She knows the truth now, no need to pretty it up. This discussion is unnecessary, there's no way she would want us now." A dull flush covered Marcus's face, and he glanced at her before looking back at the table.

He was ashamed, Devi realized, and felt tears threaten again. Ashamed that she knew his secret and he thought she would blame him. A cauldron of emotions bubbled inside of her. She needed—she didn't know what she needed. Some time. She latched on to that thought. Time would be very good to sort out everything that had happened tonight.

"I think I know what I do or don't want." Her voice rang out, clear and authoritative, and both men turned to her. Too bad she couldn't express it right now. She took a deep breath. "What I want, right this minute, is a little bit of time to think without two behemoths smashing things and yelling in my kitchen."

To their credit, both looked a little shamefaced as they glanced around the shambles of the kitchen. They had cleared the counter of all appliances and doodads, and most of it lay in pieces on the floor.

"Sorry," Marcus said gruffly. "Looks like we're nothing but trouble, huh."

In a weird way, it was like Marcus was just pushing for her to admit she wanted them gone. She figured he would rather take the disappointment now than later. She softened her tone. "It's nothing a dustpan won't take care of."

"Whatever. It's late, and I'm tired. I'm going home."

Devi frowned. When she had meant she needed a bit of time, she hadn't intended for them to leave. A flare of alarm struck her. She wanted them here, with her. She wanted to cradle them close and soothe their hurts. "You don't have to go."

Marcus wouldn't meet her eyes, but stood and walked to the doorway. "Like you said, you need some time. And so do I."

Jace laid the peas on the table. "I'll drive you home."

"Fuck you. I don't need a nursemaid." Marcus looked at her, his gaze so distant it punched her in the heart. "It's been a great week, Devi."

With that, he left, and her eyes burned as she stared at the empty doorway, the echo of the front door clicking obscenely loud. He had already said goodbye to her in his mind, she realized. He didn't think there was any way she would want him since she knew their secret.

A loud sigh brought her back to Jace, who winced as he straightened and rubbed his side. "I should follow him home. The mood he's in, he might wreck the car."

She nodded mutely and followed him to the front door. He turned and cupped a hand over her cheek. "I'm so sorry, Devi. For everything." Sadness and regret etched every line in his face.

"Are you saying goodbye too?" she whispered.

"You kidding me?" A ghost of a smile graced his lips. "I've put a lot of time and effort into this venture. I'm going to see it work if it kills me." The smile slid away. "But maybe I did rush everything. And for that I'm sorry. Me and my impatience."

"I like your impatience." She loved it. It was so Jace, to see a problem and take measured and deliberate steps to solve it.

"Yeah, well. I'm hoping I didn't screw up too badly here. Whatever you decide, Devi." Jace stroked a finger along her cheek. "Just know that I'm there for you." He dropped his hand, a flash of pain twisting his features. "And in case Marcus decides he would rather be miserable forever, I'd be honored if you'd still consider having just me in your life."

He leaned in and pressed a chaste kiss against her cheek before taking his leave. With automatic movements, she locked the door and set the alarm. She paused in the doorway of the kitchen but then moved on. *You can clean it up tomorrow.*

In the darkness of her bedroom she stripped down to her bra and panties. The set came from Marcus's purchases. Demurely cut, made of comfortable microfiber, tiny daisies danced across a background of white. With her fondness for that flower, this set was her favorite. Marcus had claimed loud and long he had bought the garments to titillate, but amongst the lace and cutaway crotches, she had also discovered comfortable cotton and whimsical designs he could only have bought with an eye toward her preferences.

In many ways, the twins knew her even better than she knew herself. She rested her head against the soft cotton of her pillow. What the hell was she going to do?

The way she looked at it, she had three options.

Number one, she could never see the twins again, and forget this week ever occurred.

Number two, she could take Jace up on his offer and leave Marcus to his own devices, thereby playing it safe. Her family would be delighted with Jace as her boyfriend.

Number three, she could say to hell with everyone else and do what her heart and body were clamoring for. Invite them both into her life. Love them both. Accept their love in return.

Her gut clenched at the thought of the first option.

The second option was more palatable, especially if Marcus was unable to work through his issues to be in a committed relationship. Jace, by himself, was a lover any woman would kill for. She knew he was probably already in love with her, and not shy about showing it. However, it would be very difficult for him to not include his brother. By the same token, there would always be a part of her yearning for Marcus, and that was hardly fair to Jace.

The third...ahh, the third was ideal. She could imagine coming home to both of them, cooking them breakfast in the morning. Kissing them off to work.

A worm of shame wiggled into her heart. Other women would have been satisfied with one man, and she would have too, before meeting Jace and Marcus. What was wrong with her that she wanted both of them forever? How could she be in love with two men? Was she abnormal?

She took comfort in the fact she couldn't imagine having

sex with anyone but them, and she had the feeling they would rip apart any other man who looked at her. They might share with each other, but no one else, and she didn't mind that.

She turned and punched her fist into the pillow. It wasn't that she thought they were the same person or anything, but often times they seemed like two sides to the same coin. She loved—yes, loved, damn it—different things about both of them. They called out to different parts of her own personality, in a way one man couldn't have done. Maybe she was just more complicated than she thought.

For a second she pictured the hazy man she had eventually assumed she would fall in love with—a doctor, maybe, or an accountant. A real accountant, not a Marcus-accountant. Someone with a paunch and a receding hairline. Someone who would be gentle and patient in the bedroom, not asking for sex more than three times a week. Someone who liked kids and puppies and never swore. They would have dinner at the same time every night and go to bed after watching the late show.

Devi shuddered in disgust. Dear Lord, she could never have that now. They had ruined her for anyone else. She pushed the covers off to the bottom of the bed and let the air-conditioning swirl over her body. It was going to be a long night.

# Chapter Fourteen

"Mr. Callahan? You have a delivery."

Marcus looked up from the papers he had spread out over his desk. For the life of him, he couldn't have told anyone what they were about, though he'd been studying them since lunchtime.

Instead of focusing on work, which he usually did with a single-minded efficiency, half of his attention was on his cell phone. For someone who hated text messages as a cultural phenomenon, he had become accustomed to Devi texting him during the past week. Usually it was nonsense. Sometimes a joke. The content didn't matter—it gave him a warm feeling to know she thought of him. Unlike Jace, he wasn't a social creature, so he didn't cultivate a huge number of friends who would casually call him during the day for no apparent reason.

He glanced at the sleek black phone lying on the desk. Today it had sat silent, with no little chirp to let him know a message had arrived.

Really, he couldn't blame her. Nobody but Jace knew his secret, and they didn't speak of it, ever. That Devi knew about his shame made him want to howl in misery. The fact that she had withdrawn didn't surprise him at all, he had expected it. What woman wanted two men, especially ones as screwed up as they were? It's not like they were a great catch.

"Mr. Callahan?"

He looked at his assistant again, who watched him with an expressionless face. Jace hated her, said she gave him the chills, but Marcus didn't mind her cold efficiency. He paid her too much for her to ask what was up with his weird behavior, and she hadn't even blinked at his black eye. "Just sign for it, Wendy."

"Yes, sir. But the delivery person said you were to open it personally."

He breathed out a sigh of irritation and motioned for her to bring it in. She stepped aside for the delivery boy, and Marcus stood, expecting an envelope. Instead, the young man came in bearing a sassy smile and a large white box with a red bow in one hand. A huge arrangement of tropical flowers was carefully cradled in the other. Marcus frowned as he studied the box and flowers the kid placed on his desk. Realizing the boy waited, he fished in his pocket and withdrew some cash.

"Hey, thanks, man."

"No problem," he muttered absently. He hadn't looked at the bill. It could have just as easily been a fifty as a five.

The door clicked quietly behind his assistant as she left. He stroked a finger along the slightly rubbery petals of the red ginger. His birthday wouldn't roll around for a few months, and as far as he knew, no one had died. He had never received flowers before, from anyone. Even Jace, as metrosexual as he was, had probably never stepped foot inside of a florist shop.

He spotted a flash of white amid the tropical colors and withdrew the card, half convinced the delivery guy had gotten the wrong person.

*Dear Marcus, when I saw these flowers, I thought of you; sometimes spiky, but beautiful, unique and hardy. Will you please be my date tonight? Be ready at six. Love, Devi*

He reread the card again, focusing on the word *Love.* In typical Devi fashion, she had scrawled a number of Xs and Os along the bottom of the line and added a smiley face.

He stroked the card before placing it on the desk with gentle reverence. He turned to the box and picked apart the bow, his fingers feeling clumsy and too big. He could have cut it, but he didn't want to damage the ribbon, which he deposited next to the card.

Once he brushed aside the tissue inside the box, he uncovered a very nice suit in his favorite color, navy blue. Labels weren't his thing, but even he could recognize an Armani when he saw it.

He sat back in his chair and stared at the box and flowers. Other than his parents and Jace no one had ever bought anything for him, especially nothing as personal as clothes. No one else had ever taken the time to shop for a gift for him, actually thinking of his tastes and personality.

He touched the spike of a bird of paradise.

What was he going to do with Devi?

"Jace, you have a delivery!"

Jace looked up at his secretary, wincing a bit from her shrill voice and singsong tone. Janice was young, the daughter of one of his associates, and since she was a single mom, he put up with her lack of professionalism and, ahem, lack of clothes. She had a good heart, and for the most part, managed to keep his office running smoothly. Although when he hadn't slept all night, it was tough not to agree with Marcus that her voice sounded like nails on a chalkboard.

Not like Devi, who always sounded melodious.

He shook his head and tried to keep his mind off her, a futile task. For the first time in a long time, he and Marcus weren't speaking. It hurt like hell, and all he wanted to do was nuzzle his face between Devi's soft breasts and let her take the pain away.

"Jacey!"

*Jace.* He gritted his teeth. "Just put it in my inbox, Janice."

She dimpled. "It's too big."

"Fine, bring it in." Sometimes he received reams of paper regarding a case he was working on, which made up a mighty hefty package. He hadn't really been expecting anything, though.

His jaw dropped when Janice came waltzing in with a large bouquet of red roses and white lilies. A gift-wrapped shoebox was wedged under her arm. "You didn't tell me it's your birthday."

"It's not." He slid back from his seat so she could place the arrangement and box on the table in front of him.

She flicked a worried glance over his face, lingering over his swollen lip. "If your significant other is trying to apologize after hurting you, I'd throw it in his face. I've dated plenty of guys like that, and once they start hitting, nothing stops them."

A dull flush covered his cheeks as he realized what she was saying. "I'm not gay, Janice."

Baby blue eyes widened. "A woman did that to you? Oh, honey, do you want the name of my self-defense instructor? A little confidence goes a long way."

"*Out*, Janice."

"But..."

"I fell, okay? Now, out."

She sniffed in outrage but stalked out the door. Jace winced, imagining her telling the entire office that he got beat up by a girl. Then his attention caught on the arrangement sitting on the table and he couldn't care less what Janice chose to tell the world.

He had received the odd gift from the girlfriend whom he happened to be with on his birthday or Christmas, but those had been shallow gifts; ties, cufflinks. Certainly no one had ever sent him flowers.

With a sense of anticipation, he reached for the card in the center of the arrangement, fearful of bruising the fragile-looking petals of the lilies.

*Dear Jace, Romance and elegance are so much your forte, I figured these flowers would suit you well. They smell as pretty as they look, and that's the way you are, just good inside and out. Will you please be my date tonight? I'll be at your place at six. Love, Devi P.S. I figured you already have tons of suits, but I noticed you eyeing these. Hope they fit.*

Choked with emotion, he stripped the paper off the box, impatient to get to the inside. Nestled in tissue lay a pair of Gucci loafers he had indeed checked out at their mall trip last week. How like Devi to have noticed. He lifted them up and looked at the size, smiling to see they were perfect.

He had just slipped them onto his feet when his cell phone chirped. Recognizing the ring, he didn't bother to check the caller ID. "Roses and lilies. Romantic and elegant. You?"

A pause. "I think they're called tropicals. Um, spiky."

Jace was startled into a laugh. "Spiky?"

Marcus cleared his throat and Jace could almost see him hunching his shoulders in embarrassment. "And unique and beautiful too," he mumbled, so fast Jace almost missed it.

"She's something."

"Yeah." Another pause. "I'm sorry I hit you."

Jace snorted. "Not as sorry as I am. Janice thinks my girl and/or gay lover smacked me around."

"Ouch. Well, maybe if you hired a secretary who isn't a casting reject from *Legally Blonde*, you might not have so many problems."

"What, so I could have a barracuda sitting in my outer office, like you? No thanks." He smiled to hear Marcus's chuckle over this familiar argument. "I'm sorry I spilled the beans."

Marcus sobered. "It's okay. I guess you didn't have much of a choice. We were getting in pretty deep."

He leaned in close to inhale a fragrant rose. "From where I'm sitting, it looks like we're still in it."

"Yeah. She's really softhearted though."

Jace knew exactly what Marcus was implying. "She might be softhearted, Marcus, but she's not soft in the head or a martyr. She wouldn't stay with a man just because she felt sorry for him."

"Mmmm." Doubt rang in the sound.

"For God's sake, man, we *do* have something to offer her too."

"You do." Shame and self-loathing laced the low words.

A sting of tears burned in Jace's eyes and for the hundredth time, he wished he could have taken Marcus's place all those years ago. "If she wanted just me, she would have said so. She wants you too. You are worthy of this. You deserve happiness. I don't know why you can't see what she and I do when we look at you."

More silence, and then Marcus spoke. "She picking you up tonight too?"

Jace closed his eyes in relief. A small doubt had remained

in the back of his mind that Devi wouldn't want both of them with her, and he was so happy it had been laid to rest. "Yeah."

"You know where we're going?"

Jace paused. He assumed her sister's party, but what if he was wrong and Devi chose not to bring them to such a public arena? She may have decided only to continue their private affair. His brother would be disillusioned, behind a veneer of indifference, of course. "Nope."

"She sent me an Armani."

A smile curved his lips. Finally, he had a comrade. Dressing Marcus qualified as a full-time job. "You don't know how gratified I am to realize you even know what that means."

"Whatever. And here I thought she was laid-back about clothes. One of you is enough."

Jace laughed. "I'll see you after work." He snapped the phone shut and snagged a rose from the arrangement, bringing it to his nose as he rested back in his chair. Amazing how ten minutes could bring about a huge change in mood and outlook. His brother and he were on speaking terms, a gorgeous woman whom he loved—that's right, loved—sent him flowers and asked him out on a potentially relationship-defining date, and he had some truly wonderful footwear on his feet. He wiggled his toes and brushed the feather-soft petals of the rose against his cheek, imagining coasting it over her curves tonight.

Everything was going his way.

# Chapter Fifteen

Devi parked her car in front of the upscale condo and took a deep breath. Thanks to her nerves, she'd suffered through a sleepless night and a tumultuous day. She should have been exhausted, but excitement and fear kept her on a razor's edge.

She stepped out onto the driveway. Typical of most Florida summer evenings, the sun still blazed in the sky despite the fact that the clock had just struck six. As she walked to the spotless white door, she wiped her hands on the back of her skirt.

In the past week, beyond that erotic encounter in Jace's bedroom, she'd only visited the twin's home as a quick stop-off to allow them to pick up clothes for the next day. Though her place was smaller, both of them seemed to prefer it. She didn't mind. Their sterile decorating scheme gave her hives.

Plus, they had the world's tiniest kitchen and barely any cooking utensils. Devi didn't know how they managed not to starve.

*Okay, focus.* She pressed the doorbell and resisted the urge to fidget. What if they hadn't received her gifts? What if they chose not to go out with her? What if Marcus had fled the country? What if... Oh.

The door opened and Marcus's wide shoulders filled the doorway. *God bless frugal living and a healthy savings account.*

The suit she had bought this morning had been worth every penny and fit him perfectly. She gave thanks he had left a spare suit at her home for the store to match in size. The dark blue set off his brooding looks and the perfect cut emphasized his build. No wonder Jace enjoyed her wearing clothes he helped pick out. A strange feeling of cavewoman possessiveness rose in her at seeing Marcus in clothes she had selected.

"Wow. You look great. I mean, you always look great, but you look really, really great." *Stop babbling.*

"Thanks."

They stared at each other for an awkward minute, and she searched for something to break the silence. "Hey, your black eye is barely noticeable."

He hunched his shoulders and muttered something.

"What?"

"I said, it's makeup. I raided my secretary's drawer after she left. I owe her some concealer, whatever the hell that is." He scowled and looked so darkly sexy she had to resist throwing herself at him.

He surveyed her from head to toe, and she was gratified by the widening of his eyes. "You look beautiful."

"Oh. This old thing." She brushed a hand against the shimmering emerald green fabric of the skirt. She had bought the beaded choli top and skirt on her last trip to India a few years ago, thinking she would lose a few pounds and be able to wear it without being self-conscious, but it had sat in the back of her closet. Today, she had forsaken the little black dress they had bought at the mall trip last week in favor of this outfit. She had known the sensual and exotic fabric would appeal to her men. Her flesh warmed where his gaze lingered on the expanse of skin revealed between the bottom of the top and the top of the skirt, on the cleavage pushed up and offered by the halter style. She didn't feel the slightest bit self-conscious, had no desire to cross her arms over her stomach or tug on fabric. Marcus and Jace spent hours worshipping her breasts and belly. How could she not feel confident?

Marcus held the door open for her and she stepped past him into their small foyer. "Do you want something to drink?"

"No, I'm okay."

"Jace is getting ready."

"It's okay, we have some time. Are you two...?"

"Cool? Yeah." He smiled sheepishly. "Sorry about your kitchen again. We haven't pounded on each other in a while. Forgot that it takes some getting used to for spectators."

"It's all right. Marcus, we didn't really get a chance to talk about everything, and—"

He raised his hand and cut her off. "Not right now, please."

She opened her mouth, but the pleading in his eyes stopped her. In any case, she had the feeling she could repeat 'til kingdom come that his past didn't bother her, and he wouldn't believe her. Marcus was a man of action, not words.

"Wow." Jace stopped on the staircase and looked down. "This is some view."

She smiled, relief making her feel briefly lightheaded at seeing Jace, just as devastatingly gorgeous in his own designer suit. The shoes she had provided looked perfect on his feet. *They're really all yours.*

"It couldn't possibly be better than the view I have."

He smiled, his eyes shining as he walked down the stairs and right up to her. He hooked a finger into the V of the top, dead center between her breasts, and pulled her close. "I want you to wear just the skirt to bed tonight," he murmured, and pressed a kiss to her mouth, his hand cupping her breast and squeezing through the fabric.

At the same time, Marcus's large hands molded against her ass. "You're an idiot. Naked is clearly the way to go."

She laughed in happiness against Jace's lips and extricated herself from their grasp. "I'll gladly wear whatever, or nothing, later. But right now, we have somewhere to be."

"As overdressed as I feel, I think we look underdressed next to you." Marcus rubbed the back of his neck. "Where are we going?"

She caught Jace's eye, and he gave an imperceptible shake of his head. So he hadn't told Marcus their likely destination tonight. She hated to keep a secret, but it would probably be more effective to keep the particulars to herself for a bit. "Um, out."

Marcus glanced between the two of them with a suspicious look. "Why do I feel like you two know something I don't?"

*Because you're too damned perceptive.* "I don't know. Oh, look at the time, we need to go." She herded them to the door, barely giving them time to turn on their house alarm. During the twenty-minute drive, she regaled them with stories about difficult customers and managed to keep their attention away from their destination until she pulled into a posh gated community.

"So where are we?" Marcus asked from the passenger seat. He frowned at the gaily lit home. The huge ranch house's long driveway was lined with cars. Since they had arrived a bit late, they parked on the street.

Devi patted her nose with the powderpuff one last time before checking her reflection critically in the pull-down mirror. "It's my mother's house."

"Your—what?" Marcus snapped his head around so fast Devi winced in sympathy.

"It's my sister's birthday party. Remember, I told you about it last week?"

"But what are we doing here?"

"We're going to attend it, Marcus," Jace spoke up from the backseat. Devi caught a definite warning in his tone.

Marcus frowned over his shoulder. "You knew about this? You two discussed this before, didn't you?"

"Well..."

"And Devi didn't want us both to come. That was the reason for the whole blowup last night."

Devi winced. Yup, too damn perceptive.

"I don't think I need to ask why the sudden turnaround, huh?" Marcus glared at her and crossed his arms over his chest. "What, did you feel so sorry for us, you had no choice? Well, fuck that. I'm not stepping foot inside that house."

"Watch your tone, Marcus," she snapped. "I don't know if I need to tattoo it on my forehead, but I don't pity you. Give me some credit."

"Don't be an ass. Sit in the car if you want to, but I'm not." Jace climbed out and opened Devi's door.

She stood slowly. Jace encircled her waist with his arm. As comforting as the gesture was, she felt miserable inside, knowing Marcus would not be joining them. She had psyched herself up for this, had reveled in the knowledge that it felt good and right.

Before Jace could close the door she leaned down so she could meet Marcus's eyes. "I'm sorry I didn't tell you earlier. But I truly want to be here with you tonight. I would be so proud to be on your arm."

"So people can gossip?"

"At the end of the day, I'm concerned first about what I

think of myself, and then what you and Jace think of me. Everyone else comes in a very distant third."

"You tell yourself that now."

She lifted a shoulder in a tiny shrug. "And I'll tell you that next week, and next month, and next year. But I guess that's how it is when you're in love with someone."

Marcus inhaled, and his eyes glittered in the waning light. "You're confusing lust with love."

"If you choose to believe that, fine." She tossed the car keys on the seat and closed the door. "Ball's in your court now."

Her lack of tears made her proud, but each step away from the car was harder than she had believed possible, even with Jace at her side. He squeezed her hand. "He'll come around, sweetheart."

She gave him a sad smile. "I hope so. For all our sakcs."

They arrived at the front door and she tried to focus on the present. She brushed some imaginary lint off his shoulder. "Ready to run the gauntlet?"

"For you? Any time."

She took a deep breath and pressed the doorbell.

"And then I said, what's the point? She'll sue someone else next week." A loud burst of laughter from the crowd around Jace made Devi smile from where she stood next to her mother.

"Devi, why didn't you tell me you were seeing someone? And he's so sweet." Devi breathed a sigh of relief at her mother's softly accented praise. Her parents had immigrated to America in the seventies, and while she had never come right out and said it, Devi knew her slightly old-school parent dreamed of Indian son-in-laws, preferably ones she handpicked. Devi loved Mama deeply, though often it seemed as if Leena and Rana mothered her more. Mama had always been a little absent from their lives—first running the business when they were young, and now with all her charitable boards. Rana claimed this was a good thing. While Mama indulged and left her and Leena to their own devices, she remained sharply critical of her eldest daughter's choices and flamboyance.

"I'm glad you like him," Devi answered.

"Are you kidding me? Everyone loves him."

True to form, Jace had managed to charm everyone he met, paying special attention to her mother and Leena.

"I just knew she had someone on the line," Leena bragged as she walked up, her eyes twinkling. "She's been wearing makeup and clothes that actually fit her body."

Her mother gasped in mock surprise. "No!"

"I know, and then she has the nerve to be surprised with all the compliments she's received tonight."

Both of them laughed, and Devi rolled her eyes but stood up straighter. She had been receiving a huge number of compliments tonight, and she knew the reason didn't lie in her clothes, but the sudden boost of inner confidence she must be transmitting. Before, she had always felt hidden and out of the way. Now she was aware of her effect on people. Men openly admired, much to Jace's whispered mock dismay, and women watched her with covetous eyes. After a lifetime of living in the shadows, it felt rather good.

"Hey, is Rana here yet?"

Leena's question put a bit of a damper on Devi's mood, and their mama's too, if her tightened lips were any indication. "If that girl shows up with that tattooed lowlife I saw her with last week, I will insist she leave my house."

"Mama, not tonight, okay? That girl is your daughter too."

A dark shadow moved in their mother's face and she remained silent, lines of disappointment making her look much older than a handsome woman in her mid-fifties should.

Devi rested on pins and needles, waiting for Rana as well, since her arrival would drop the other figurative shoe. Like a coward, she had half-hoped that Leena would have spoken with Rana last night after meeting Jace, thus learning the truth early and sparing them a scene here tonight, but no luck. Well, she would just have to take it as it came.

She shifted, uncomfortably aware of someone watching her. She took a sip of the punch in her hand and searched through the gaily dressed crowd.

Marcus's height made him easy to spot. Her breath caught. "Um, excuse me. There's someone I need to see."

She made her way through the dancers, uncaring and unnoticing of those who hailed her, until she stood in front of him. "Hi."

"Hi."

She inhaled his scent. "I am so happy you're here."

A small smile graced his mouth. "I think you're crazy to feel that way."

"Tough. They're my feelings."

He shoved his hands in his pockets and glanced around. "Nice party. Seemed stupid to sit in a car for hours when I could be in here scarfing down appetizers and dancing with a beautiful woman." The music segued into a slow dance and Marcus bowed formally over her hand, charming her. "Would you do me the honors?"

She walked with him to the dance floor and they slipped

into the group of swaying couples. “Dancing with just one woman? Surely you’d get bored.”

“There’s only one woman I see who’s worth dancing with. Who’s worth going home to.” He stepped in closer, his breath brushing across her face. “Did you mean what you said?”

She didn’t pretend to misunderstand, and she didn’t need to think twice. Love for him beat through her veins. “Yes.”

“It’s only been a week.”

“Sometimes all it takes is a day.”

“And it’s not because of what Jace told you?”

She rested her head against his chest, where she could feel the thump of his heart. She had the feeling she would need to repeat this again and again, until Marcus truly believed her. His pride was enormous. “I feel bad for the little boys you were. But my love is for the wonderful men you’ve become.”

It was too much to hope Marcus would say “I love you” back to her right now, but she didn’t mind waiting. Marcus cleared his throat. “I still think you’re crazy. And Jace and I must be too.”

“Then let’s be crazy together.” To her surprise, Marcus danced the waltz with grace and expertise. “Where did you learn to dance?”

“My mom made us learn when we were kids. Jace and I had to actually take turns being the woman. It was very emasculating.”

She laughed and rested her head against him. Over his shoulder, she caught a glimpse of Jace, still engaged with a large knot of people. He nodded in response to the chattering man at his side, but he watched them, a small, satisfied smile on his face. He inclined his head in a salute, and she wiggled her fingers and grinned back at him.

The dance ended all too soon, and Devi and Marcus stood staring at each other with goofy smiles before the jostling around them forced them off the dancc floor. *God, I just want to get him home and kiss him all over...*

"*Devi.*" Leena's voice caught her attention. Marcus had his back to her sister, but Devi could see Leena over his shoulder clearly. Her, and the woman clad in shimmering black she towed in her wake. "There you are. I wanted to introduce Rana to your new boyfriend."

# Chapter Sixteen

To be fair, Rana's eyes didn't exactly bug out when Marcus turned around, but it was close. Very close.

"I told you our baby sister had a secret boyfriend. This is Jace." Leena looked him up and down with a small frown. "Weren't you wearing a different suit?"

"I'm not Jace, I'm his brother, Marcus." Marcus gave both women a smile so blinding, Devi blinked. He shook hands with Leena and nodded to Rana. "I believe we met last week at the restaurant?"

Rana looked shell-shocked, but she nodded, her large chandelier earrings making a musical tinkling noise.

Devi licked her lips. "Leena, Marcus is also..."

A sharp squeeze on her elbow surprised and silenced her. "Delighted to be here. Thank you so much for inviting me, as well." He looked around at the crush of people. "When you guys throw a party, you go all out, huh?"

"Oh, there's nothing Indians love more than an excuse to dress up and party." Leena laughed. "Well, Jace didn't mention you guys were twins." Her sharp eyes flickered over Marcus's bare left hand, and a crafty gleam shone. "So you already know Rana? Hey, Rana, why don't you show Marcus where the bar is?"

"It's on the left wall—ouch."

Leena's determined smile couldn't hide the pinch she had just administered. "It's so crowded, why don't you take him there?"

Devi inwardly winced and cast an apologetic look at Marcus. No one could accuse Leena of subtlety.

"I'm not interested in him, okay, Leena?" Rana blurted out.

Well, maybe she could sign both her sisters up for diplomacy lessons.

"Rana." Leena's admonishment was followed by Marcus's chuckle-turned-cough.

"Leena." The low-pitched masculine voice oozed oily charm. Leena's long-time boyfriend, Rahul, stepped up behind her and took her arm. "I wanted to introduce you to some people and you disappeared." He nodded to Devi and Rana but ignored Marcus.

Devi smiled but didn't bother to speak. As darkly handsome and wealthy as Rahul was, she'd never liked him, and she knew Rana didn't either. He didn't do or say anything untoward, and their mother adored him, but she got a bad feeling whenever he came around.

Perhaps, Devi noted, watching Leena's expressive face wipe clean of emotion, it was the way her normally assertive and energetic sister acted around him, like a shadow of herself. "I'll be there in a second."

"These are important people, Leena."

She blew out a huff of air. Devi's eyes widened over Leena expressing even that much displeasure with her boyfriend. "Okay." She flashed them a strained smile and spoke to Marcus. "Please, grab a drink and enjoy your night."

Marcus nodded. Rana barely waited until Leena had left

hearing range before she whirled on them. "What the fuck is going on here?"

"Hi, Rana. It's good to see you again." Jace materialized by Devi's right side and flanked her. Devi had no doubt he'd been watching, waiting to see if they would need backup.

Her sister shot him a dirty look. "Excuse me if I'm not delighted to see the two of you here. Are you kidding me?" She lowered her voice and leaned in close to Devi. "Baby, when I introduced you to these two, I thought you were just going to use them to get out of your rut. I never intended for you to see them again, let alone bring them to a family function."

"That's rather shortsighted of you." Jace rocked back on his heels. "I do come to your restaurant on a fairly regular basis. Were you going to ban me?"

"I was prepared to lose a regular customer to jumpstart my sister's sex life."

"And isn't this great? Now you don't have to lose me."

Rana's eyes narrowed to slits. "What kind of game are you two playing?"

"No game." Marcus spoke up. "Trust me."

Rana snorted. "Yeah, right. Devi, come with me, we need to talk."

"No."

"What?"

She swallowed. Rana's surprise almost equaled her own. She had never blatantly disobeyed her oldest sister. "I don't need an intervention. And I don't need you to protect me from myself this time."

Rana rolled her eyes. "You and I both know you aren't a good judge of men."

"Well, there you go. You should be thrilled. You picked Jace and Marcus."

"For one night, not—"

"How long I choose to be with them is my decision, not yours. I won't let you mess this up for me."

"They're players, just like Tarek. You remember how much he hurt you?"

Devi's grip on her temper slipped. "They are nothing like Tarek. They are good, decent men. You could offer yourself to them naked and they wouldn't even look at you twice if they had made a commitment to me."

Rana snorted. "You're fooling yourself."

"No, I'm not. I'll never worry that I'll walk in on them with another woman, not like I did with you and Tarek."

A silence descended over the four of them, frozen in a tableau amidst the revelry. Marcus was the first to speak. "You slept with her boyfriend?" Disgust rang heavy in his voice, and his lip curled.

Her face white but for the garish red stripe of her lipstick, Rana shot him a look containing a shadow of her normal sassiness. "You're one to talk."

"They never had sex." Devi spoke in a low voice. "It was arranged for me to walk in on them making out on my sofa."

"She wouldn't listen to us. We told her he was hitting on anything in a skirt, but we knew she wouldn't believe it until she saw it." Rana studied her with pain in her eyes. "She was talking marriage, and I couldn't let her do that. She knows how sorry I am, that I never meant anything by it. *Tell* them."

Devi frowned at her. "Of course I know that, Rana. I forgave you the minute you explained what happened. I never blamed you."

Rana laughed, a hollow sound. "Saint Devi. You should

have. God knows I've blamed myself enough."

"I know," she explained gently. "Which is why I could never bring myself to. You need to get over this guilt. It's really unwarranted."

"How can I when I seem to have put something else in motion?" Rana studied the three of them. "What exactly is all of this about?"

Devi thought for a minute. "Love."

If anything, Rana looked even more tortured, tears shining in her eyes. "Oh dear Lord, what have I done? That's impossible. Please, just come with me, and we can go talk it over with Leena."

Devi leaned against Marcus, who put a solid arm around her. Jace stroked his fingers down her wrist until he gripped her hand securely. Their support gave her the strength to stand up to her sister. "No, Rana. I don't need to talk anything over. Please, for once, just trust me to know my own mind."

Rana opened her mouth, but their mother's voice intruded. "Well, I see you finally decided to show up. I hope you don't have a drunken lover around to crash this party like you did at your graduation."

Rana cast her an impatient glance. "Not now, Mother."

Mama raised a thinly plucked eyebrow. "I see you've at least met Devi's new young man. I do hope you're behaving yourself." She smiled at Marcus. "And of course you must be Jace's brother."

As soon as their mother had appeared, Marcus had withdrawn his arm from around Devi, and she mourned its loss. "Mrs. Malik. How do you do? I can see where Devi gets her looks. How can there be a whole family of such attractive women?"

Rana rolled her eyes but Mama giggled. "And I can see charm runs in your family."

"Honesty, ma'am. Hardly charm."

Mama smiled, though it slipped when she turned to Rana. "Can you please come with me? I need to speak with you about these caterer friends of yours."

"Actually, Devi and I just needed to chat about something..."

"No, she doesn't. I mean, we don't," Devi interjected quickly. "You go on and handle your catering crisis."

Mama inclined her head regally. "Okay, baby. A pleasure to meet both of you."

Marcus and Jace murmured their goodbyes as Mama dragged Rana away. Rana twisted to look over her shoulder. *Later,* she mouthed.

As soon as they were gone, Marcus rubbed circles onto her back, and she sagged into Jace's support, grateful to have both their hands on her. "Well, that went...well."

"Mmmm."

She turned to Marcus. "Why didn't you let me tell Leena what was going on? She's going to find out."

He shrugged. "I knew it would be uncomfortable for you, and you don't have to prove anything to me. Anyway, the more people who know, the more gossip. I don't want people to talk about you. If I have to take a second seat out in public, that's cool." Marcus grinned. "I've never been one for public displays of affection anyway."

Devi raised an eyebrow. "Unless it's in a dressing room, huh?"

Jace chuckled and drew her closer. "No, he's serious. Me, on the other hand." He kissed the side of her neck, the brief pass of his tongue sending tingles through her skin. “I can’t resist touching you and I don’t care who sees.”

Devi shivered and leaned into Jace’s kiss. She’d done her duty, proven her point. Time to get her men out of here and introduce them to the rest of her plans for the night. “Our normal baker wasn’t available. The sweets aren’t really up to your standards.”

Jace drew back and raised an arrogant brow. “Yeah?”

“So it’s really not necessary to stay for the cake.”

Marcus crowded closer to her. “I can pass on the cake, if you can make me a better offer.”

“Well, you know, technically, I am wearing a skirt.” She sent them both what she hoped was a sultry look. “And we know how good I am at following your rules.”

Marcus’s eyes widened and then narrowed in rising lust and realization. “Home, now.”

“Ahh, there’s the growl I love so much,” she teased as he grabbed her hand and navigated through the maze of couples. “I was wondering where that polite and charming man had come from.”

“I’m charming...around everyone but you,” he admitted. “You just make me feel too raw to worry about charm.”

“Lucky for you, I don’t mind.”

“Yeah. Lucky me.”

# Chapter Seventeen

The car ride passed in relative quiet as Devi drove to her house. At some point Jace, who sat next to her, switched the radio on to a soulful jazz station. Appropriately, fat drops of rain started to hit her windshield just as she took the exit off the thruway.

None of them said or did anything sexual, but the combination of the saxophone, the rain and their hulking presence in the car worked as effectively as an hour of foreplay. By the time Devi pulled into her driveway, she was ready to jump onto the nearest male. Her gaze met Jace's and he shook his head slowly, a gleam in his eyes. "No. Inside."

She licked her lips and clambered out of the car, feeling graceless and clumsy. Her car chirped as she locked it, and she placed the key ring in Marcus's outstretched hand. Her nerves were too rattled to handle them appropriately.

They entered the foyer behind Devi, and she waited with eyes downcast for one of them to grab her from behind and press her against the wall.

Seconds stretched into a full minute, and she looked over her shoulder with a frown. Where were her take-charge men?

Both of them stood inside the door, shadows covering their faces, arms crossed over their chests. A dizzying rush went through Devi. In the dark, they looked so identical, she didn't think she could tell them apart.

"What are you guys waiting for?"

The one on the left answered. "This is your show, sweetheart."

She turned. Their voices were similar, but she thought by the tone and endearment the speaker might be Jace. Her show. Now that was interesting.

She flipped on one of the switches that lit a recessed light right above her. The floodlight shone a spot of illumination on her, while casting Jace and Marcus even further into shadows.

Her hips swayed to the music of the rain pounding on her roof. She should have felt a bit ridiculous—strip-teasing wasn't really her forte—but the bubble cocooning the three of them didn't allow for feelings of self-consciousness.

She raised her arms and her fingers found the knot of the halter tie behind her neck with fingers no longer clumsy. She worked it free and the ties dropped down. The fabric of the top caught on her nipples. The hook-and-eye closures lower on her back were easier to deal with and the garment opened. She held it to her front before allowing it to slip to the floor, baring her breasts. She stroked a finger down a slope, over a tightening nipple, her head falling back.

A sharp inhale from the left prompted a slight smile. So it had been Jace. She knew he had a special affinity for her breasts. Marcus, on the other hand, appreciated another body part far more.

She turned her back to the twins, feeling two pairs of eyes roving over the smooth expanse of her back. The zipper on the side of her skirt took a second to undo, and the fabric fell to her feet in a quiet whisper of silk. She arched her back.

"Fuck."

"Shit."

The swear words were said with all the reverence of someone at worship. "Were you wearing this all night?" The hard voice came from right behind her, so she wasn't surprised when she felt Marcus's hand rest on her ass.

She cast a sultry look over her shoulder. "Of course," she purred. "I wanted to be ready for you."

His face tightened even more, and he led her to the wall, pressing her forward with a hand on the middle of her back until she stood with her palms flush to the hard drywall, her back arched. He inserted a foot between hers and pushed them apart. With a gentle hand, he touched the base of the butt plug she had inserted earlier.

"Is this the biggest one?"

Over the past week, Devi had become accustomed to taking the dildos as they fucked her, until she had come to crave the time when they finally judged her ready to take their cocks up that tight channel.

"Answer me." Marcus punctuated the demand by sliding the plug in an inch and then out again.

"Yes," she gasped, though the resulting sensation was almost too much for her to bear.

He cupped his palm over the base of the plug. "I wish I could do this to you. Just stay inside you all day so you would feel me when you were eating and working and sleeping."

"That would be...wonderful."

"But since I'm with you now, we don't need this, do we?" Marcus gripped the base of the plug and withdrew it so slow she felt every little nuance of the hard plastic. The muscles in her anus clenched hard, reluctant to let that wonderful source of fullness vanish.

Marcus chuckled. "You're too greedy, little girl."

"No such thing." Jace spoke from behind her, and his palm settled over the base of her spine, holding her steady. She knew he watched his brother remove the plug and her pussy grew wetter than the plug itself had made her.

The plug popped free and Marcus tossed it to the carpet before gripping her wrist and turning her around. Lightning flashed and threw his face, lined with lust, into stark relief. "Where?"

*Her show.* "Bedroom." The couch was closer, no doubt, but she had a feeling this was too important an encounter not to have it take place in her bed.

He nodded and picked her up in his arms. She released a little shriek of surprise before she clenched her fingers around his thick biceps. The way these two hauled her around, she felt as though she weighed less than nothing.

When they entered the room, Jace crossed to the large window and jerked the curtains apart so the fury and noise of the storm had a front-row seat to their coupling. Marcus tossed her on the bed, and she settled with a bounce on the soft mattress. "No light this time?" she tried to joke.

"Storms are sexy. The lightning will give us any light we need. Besides, I can see your body with just my hands now." Jace shrugged out of his jacket and dropped it carelessly on the floor, which told her more than anything how eager he was for her. He walked closer to the bed, unfastening his cuff links as he strolled.

She licked her lips and realized Marcus mirrored his movements as he undressed, both attacking the buttons of their shirts and then unzipping and sliding their pants down muscular legs.

She *was* greedy. She wanted to climb all over them, lay

them on a table and gorge herself on them. Even then she knew she would never be full.

Jace was the first to finish undressing, and he climbed over her like a sleek panther, all lean muscles and barely checked hunger. His cock rose thick and hard between his legs. He kissed her passionately, but grabbed the hand she slid down between their bodies before she could brush against the moisture already escaping from his penis. He pinned her other wrist to the bed, leaving her helpless in his grasp. "We're already on the edge. Don't push me over."

"I thought this was my show?"

Jace smiled. "You do your name proud. It means goddess, right?"

Devi looked up in surprise. "How did you know that?"

"I Googled it. Forgive me, goddess. I only want to worship your body." He leaned down and nipped at her breast. He looked up at her through lowered lashes. "Do you really want me to let you go?"

The seduction in his voice should have warned her, but still, when he pulled her nipple into his mouth and sucked hard, she arched off the bed. His hands on her wrists bowed her body, and she cried out in impatience.

He let go of her nipple for a brief second. "Should I let go?"

She strained against his bond. No. She loved being held down, needed something to brace herself against. She shook her head.

Nonetheless, he freed her wrists and guided her hands to the rails of the headboard. "Hang on tight."

Devi clenched her fingers around the poles, as Jace sucked and licked his way down her body. He settled between her thighs and gripped her legs behind her knees to pull them up.

Before she could become self-conscious, two fingers on her jaw turned her head to the side.

Marcus stood by the side of the bed, his large cockhead on perfect level with her mouth. She opened her mouth and drew him in, savoring the salty taste of his body, just as Jace's tongue lapped at her pussy.

The sensations that exploded through her body were indescribable as Jace settled in, as if to savor her. He flattened his tongue over her clitoris and she arched up, dislodging him and Marcus from her mouth.

Low growls emerged from both of them as they brought her back into position. Marcus wrapped his hand around the base of his cock and slipped the head between her lips. His shallow thrusts mimicked the teasing licks between her legs. She looked up to see Marcus staring at his brother's head between her legs, sweat beading along his hairline. She released the headboard to sink her fingers into his buttocks in silent demand. He switched his gaze to her. "You want more?" She nodded, her mouth stuffed. He cradled his hands around her skull and pressed his thumbs against her cheeks, so the silken lining caressed his hard cock as he thrust. He shuddered, and thankfully, spoke for her. "Do it harder, man. Our Devi isn't satisfied."

Jace lifted her legs until they pressed against her body, giving himself open access. His head bobbed between her legs in rapid jabs, and Marcus sped up as well. The coil of tension knotted harder with every thrust, until...

Until both men released her, Marcus withdrawing from her mouth and Jace rising on his knees from between her legs. "What? Don't stop, please."

Jace slipped just the tips of two fingers inside of her pussy, and she writhed, trying to draw him deeper. Her juice gleamed on his mouth as he smiled. "We'll make you feel good in just a second, baby."

Were they crazy? "Now!" She clambered to sit up and crawled toward him. He laughed as she straddled his lap, his heavily veined cock pressed right against her soaking pussy. She tried to coax him into her body, but he stopped her by the expedient method of holding on to her hips.

"Wait. Wait, Devi. Condom." He had to repeat himself to pierce through her haze of desire.

She shook with arousal, but tried to wait the two seconds it took him to roll the latex down his hard cock. She resented the barrier, though she knew she would appreciate his thoughtfulness later. The instant he completed the chore, she tried to direct him toward her needy pussy, but he stopped her again. She shook in frustration. "What are you waiting for?"

Jace looked over her shoulder. Her nightstand drawer closed with a thud behind her and an open tube of lubrication landed next to them on the bed. His gaze returned to hers and he smiled mischievously. "That."

Without further ado, he lay back on the bed and had her straddle him. Through with foreplay, she seated him in one thrust, her back arching in pleasure. She tried to raise herself up for another bone-rattling thrust, but hands on her back pushed her down until she lay pinned against Jace's chest, her bottom high in the air.

Two heavily lubricated fingers stretched into her ass, and she froze in a moment of apprehension. It was one thing to take toys and fingers, but would she be able to take Marcus in that small hole?

She didn't get much of a chance to consider it, though, since his fingers withdrew. She looked over her shoulder as Jace placed both of his hands on her cheeks and spread her open. Marcus's nostrils flared. He glanced up to meet her apprehensive gaze. "Don't worry, baby. I'm going to make you feel so good."

"I'll help," Jace whispered near her ear, distracting her for the split second Marcus needed to press his cock against her rear entrance and pop inside her. She moaned. The pain was there, yes, but there was also a terrible emptiness. She wanted more than just the inch or so Marcus had thrust in. She tightened her muscles, bearing down at Jace at the same time. "No, baby. Loosen up. Relax and take a breath and let Marcus work it in. Won't it feel good when we're both inside of you? You're going to feel so stuffed. There's nothing that feels as good as this." He groaned as she relaxed, listening to him speak. Marcus pressed deeper, and she started to pant, wanting nothing more than to writhe between them.

When she tried to move, though, Marcus's hand snapped against her ass. The smack only drove her passion higher. "Please!"

A low chuckle resounded from Marcus's chest where it pressed against her back. "You're such a bad girl, Devi. What are we going to do with you?"

Her head tossed. "Fuck me the way I need it."

Marcus growled and thrust hard into her ass until his belly rested against her lower back. For an instant, they all froze, and then Jace gasped. "Fuck, you're so tight."

He started to thrust beneath her, and Marcus helped her to sit up a bit so he could slide his hands between them. He gripped her breasts to hold her steady, and then he too started to thrust behind her.

Their rhythm was perfect so she never felt empty. Their thrusts became more frenzied, and Devi felt like a vessel tossed about in a sea. The only thing keeping her moored were their hands on her breasts and ass.

"Shit, I'm not going to last." Jace threw his head back and gritted his teeth. "Devi—love you."

The words set off her own climax, and she clenched down on Marcus's hardness until he roared his release. "Fuck. Love you. Fucking love you," he gasped in her ear.

He collapsed on top of her, and the sweat fused them together as one entity. She shifted as the air cooled their heated bodies down, and she yawned, too exhausted to move. "I love you guys too."

Marcus's hand clenched on her hip and Jace brushed a kiss against her temple, the only sign that they had even heard. She didn't know how long they lay there, but in the cocoon of darkness and rain, everything was right with her world. Everything was just where it belonged.

Sometime later, Marcus urged her up and they slipped her into a bath, taking turns stroking a loofah over her tired body. Over the past week, Jace had been the one to guide her into a warm bath or clean her up after they had devastated her sexually. The fact that Marcus was also here, in the tub, tonight, was significant. If only she wasn't so extremely tired, she'd be able to figure out what the significance was.

A slight sexual tingling rose in her body when Jace rubbed over her breasts, but he shook his head firmly, and she didn't have the energy to argue with them.

Like a child, they tenderly dried her off and slipped a pair of panties up her legs—probably to work as some sort of chastity belt, she mused with loopy amusement—before they guided her back into her bed. She crawled in, curling between their bodies. Jace cupped her breast in his hand and immediately spooned around her back in his favorite position.

Though he had stayed to bathe her, Devi half expected Marcus to roll out of bed as usual and go sleep on her couch.

Instead, he faced her and brushed a caress over her stomach before he curled his arm around her and dragged her closer until he could rest a heavy leg over hers. Jace murmured a protest before he followed and slipped his leg between hers, his arm just over Marcus's. Front to back and all around, she felt their skin and their breath, and it felt so good, she drifted into a doze immediately.

Yes, everything was just perfect.

# Chapter Eighteen

The ringing escalated until Devi tossed her head restlessly and reached out to slap at the offending alarm clock.

"Oof."

Instead of cold plastic, her hand landed on a truly hot set of ripped abs. Unable to stop herself, she clenched her fingers and kneaded hard flesh, before she slid down to rapidly hardening morning wood. A hand snaked over her ass, conveniently accessible by her facedown position. *Now this is the way to wake up.*

Marcus groaned. "What the fuck is that noise?"

Yeah, come to think of it, her alarm played a nice pop-rock station in the mornings. Never that shrill ringing.

And when had her clock started up that pounding noise? Weird.

"The door," she blurted out and rose on her hands and knees before sitting up. A hank of hair fell into her eyes and she batted at it. "Someone's at the door."

"Who comes to your door at eight on a weekend?" Marcus grumbled.

"I don't know." Concern set in, and she clambered out of bed.

Jace levered himself up, irritation in every sleepy line of his face. "Come back to bed and let Marcus handle it."

"Why me?" Marcus groaned.

"'Cause I need Devi."

"I need her too."

She rolled her eyes and grabbed the terrycloth robe off the back of the door. "Both of you stay here. I do have elderly neighbors, and the last thing I need is them dropping dead of a heart attack at a naked man answering my door."

The ringing stopped and Jace's face brightened. "See, they're gone. Come back to bed."

She tightened the belt on her robe as the pounding started up again. "I'll handle this and be right back."

"Hell, Devi, we only came once last night." Marcus folded his arms over his chest. His bare, tanned, muscular chest. His lickable, suckable...

Devi forced her gaze away and made her feet move out the door. "I'll call the Guinness Book on the way back. I'm sure they'll be interested. Now, stay."

"Five minutes..."

She wasn't sure who the warning came from as she securely closed the door, but her smile faded as she moved to the front door, which was almost vibrating from the force of the knocker's fist.

She frowned in real concern as she undid the deadbolt and cracked the door open. The door flew out of her hands and she took a startled step back as a black-haired tempest hurtled in.

"Where are they?"

Devi swore the shout rattled the chandelier, and she stared at Leena standing in her foyer, arms akimbo. Her normally meticulously groomed sister wore a ratty baby T-shirt and paint-spattered shorts. Not a trace of makeup covered her face.

A messy topknot secured her hair in a bundle on top of her head, and it wobbled with every move she made. She looked like an infuriated, dark-haired hen.

"Leena, what's wrong?"

"What's wrong?" Leena glared at her. "I'll tell you what's wrong. What's wrong is that I was supposed to be sleeping off my hangover when this one"—she pointed to Rana, who quietly entered the foyer and closed the door behind her—"comes and wakes me up to tell me a fantastic story about identical twins and threesomes and *love*. Two of those three things should never be used in the same sentence. So, I'm going to ask you again. Where are they?"

After shooting a quick glare at Rana, who looked down at her feet, Devi crossed her arms over her chest and stared Leena down. "None of this is any of your business."

"None of my business? You're my business. You and your abominable taste in men." She held up her hand and ticked off the points on her fingers. "There was that biker guy back in high school. Then the 'artist' in college. Then Tarek. Face it. You're mush in the wrong man's hands. You're a ridiculous romantic who idealizes every man you so much as kiss. You need to be protected from yourself."

Devi took the verbal slap with only a slight flinch. She had suspected their opinions, but how odd to hear it spoken aloud, that her sisters felt she was an imbecile just waiting to be conned by a big strong man, or men. "And you two are jaded cynics. I admit I've been mistaken about men in the past, but I'm not a total idiot." She ticked off each man on her own fingers, mimicking Leena. "The biker was a conscious decision, my own stupid rebellion. The artist I was getting sick of supporting way before you found him that job in Cali you thought I knew nothing about, Leena. I would have kicked him to the curb soon enough. I didn't feel so bad for his tortured soul that I would have wasted my life on him." She shook her head sharply when Leena opened her mouth, and continued. "And, as for Tarek..." Devi looked at Rana. "Rana, did you know why I wasn't madder at you?" Rana shook her head. "Because two days before I'd found lipstick on his collar and some amateur porn photos of him and some slut fucking on my bed. Unfortunately, he had talked me into opening a joint bank account with him, and I didn't want to kick him to the curb before I disentangled my money from his. I knew he was a snake enough to try to run off with my stuff. So you see, I was leaving him anyway."

Rana's face turned white, her lips pinched together. "Why didn't you tell me?"

"Because you were already so torn up about it." Devi gave her a half smile. "Really, I didn't see the point in telling you your sacrifice was completely unnecessary."

Rana's laugh was more of a sob. "Saint Devi. You would be thinking of my feelings."

"Well, this is all very interesting," Leena snapped, her eyes glittering. "But excuse me if I'm still not convinced. I'm guessing your two boy toys are still in the bedroom?"

"Nope, her boy toys are right here."

Jace's determinedly cheerful voice froze her to her spot, as did the two arms sliding around her waist in opposite directions as they flanked her. She cast her eyes heavenward. *Please let them be dressed.*

A quick glance assured her that Jace had indeed pulled on his slacks, while Marcus had slid into his Jockey boxer-briefs. The snug-fitting cotton and the expanse of bare skin didn't really do much to help her focus, but she managed to tear her gaze away from the bulge in his crotch.

Leena drew herself up to her full height. Even mussed and casually dressed, she was intimidating. “I don’t know what kind of game you sickos are playing, but—”

“Oh, we play lots of games,” Jace said earnestly. “Personally, I like the one where we’re patrolmen who pull over this sexy speeder...”

Devi blinked and spoke before she recalled their guests. “Hey, we never played that.”

Marcus tightened his fingers around her waist. “That’s ’cause we haven’t gotten a chance to buy any handcuffs.” He looked at her sisters and raised his eyebrows. “We wore out our last ones.”

She stifled a snort of laughter at their provoking behavior but lost amusement at Leena’s glower. “Okay, boys, enough.” She stepped forward. “Leena, Rana, while I appreciate your concern, what’s between Jace, Marcus and I is our concern, not yours.”

“It is my concern, if you fuck up your life with a couple of perverts.” She surprised Devi by grabbing hold of her arm. Devi winced at the biting grip and Marcus stood in front of her in an instant. He broke the hold and tossed Leena’s hand down. His shoulders wonderfully wide, he leaned down and stuck his face right in Leena’s.

“You don’t ever touch her again in anger. Ever.”

Leena opened her mouth and then closed it again before her chin firmed. Even that small sign of weakness coming from her indomitable sister surprised Devi. “For Christ’s sake, I wouldn’t have hurt her. She’s my baby sister. I love her.”

“And so do we.” Jace pushed Marcus to the side. “We would never hurt her either.”

Devi worked herself through the wall of muscle until she stood between them again. “They aren’t perverts, Leena.”

Leena sneered. “Then what would you call it?”

“Pleasure. Love. Sharing. Pleasure we need.” Jace looked down at Devi, a slight question in his eyes. “Pleasure Devi needs too.”

Devi nodded immediately, glad to see the doubt vanish. She needed them, no doubt. No one man would be able to quench her sexuality the way these two had shown her. And she would never be able to have sex with just any two men. Only Jace and Marcus.

“And you don’t call that perverted?”

Jace shrugged. “I can’t believe that any sister of Devi has a completely vanilla sex life. Or if she does, I can’t imagine she’s happy in it.”

“My sex life is my business, jackass.”

Like the lawyer he was, Jace pounced. “And Devi’s is her own.” He cocked his head, his eyes kind but sharp. “So you’ll leave her to it without making any nasty slurs or sneering remarks, but trust that she knows her own mind and she knows what will make her happy. I imagine that’s what a good sister would do.”

Leena studied them and then blew out a breath. “I don’t even know why I’m getting my blood pressure up. It’s not like this is going to last forever. I give you another week, Devi. Maybe two, ’cause you’re so damn loyal.”

Devi gritted her teeth. Would her sisters ever think she was more than a blindly devoted puppy? “You’re wrong.”

“Whatever.” Leena stalked out the open door. “Come on, Rana.”

Instead of following, Rana stood in her position just inside the foyer. “I’m really sorry, Devi.”

Devi shrugged, though her heart was heavy. She hated

fighting with her sisters. "You did what you thought best. The two of you always do."

"It's not us against you. I can see how you might think that right now. But you have to know that we love you so much."

"I know. And your love is the only reason I've forgiven you guys in the past for your meddling. But now, I just need you to trust in me."

"Okay."

"Because, really, we... What?" Devi stopped and stared.

Rana shrugged. "I admit, I was worried, but honestly, Devi, I've never seen you actually fight for anything before. If this is what you want, then I won't argue with you anymore. I'd rather have my baby sister talking to me with two boyfriends than not at all." The car honked and she rolled her eyes before stepping away from the wall. "Leena will come around. But you may want to wait a while—like, never—before you break the news to Mama." Rana's lips twisted wryly. "She's indulgent with you because she knows we look out for you, but if she finds out about this, trust me, you'll be judged and tarred and feathered as a whore before you can blink. No one knows that better than me."

"No one thinks you're a whore."

"Baby, you may not, but Mama's been convinced since I broke curfew at the tenth-grade spring fling." Rana made a dismissive motion, though her eyes filled with pain. "Whatever." She looked between Jace and Marcus. "Jace, you remember what I told you I would do if you hurt Devi? You know, how I'd cut off your balls and feed them to you?"

"Jesus, Rana..."

Jace's lips quirked. "How could I forget?"

Rana smiled sweetly and stepped outside the door. "If you

hurt her, I'll still feed them to you. But I think I might keep them attached to your body when I do it."

Marcus flinched, no doubt reconsidering his coming to this powwow in just a pair of underwear. He continued to stare after her sister as she closed the door. "Those are some tough bitches."

"Hey, now." She elbowed him, and it was rather like elbowing a chunk of granite. "Those are my sisters. Clean up your language."

He grasped her around her waist and tugged her closer so they faced each other. "I didn't mean any offense. I admire tough bitches. Like you. Look at you, facing down the opposition in the name of love."

Devi pursed her lips. "I don't think anyone's ever called me a bitch before." Hmm, now that she thought of it, she'd rather be a bitch than a wuss.

"Yeah," Jace said from behind her, his tone wry. "Marcus has a unique courting style." He slipped his arms around her and rested his chin on her head.

She twisted her head to the side to look up at him. "So where do we go from here?"

"Well, that kind of depends on you. You are an integral part of this, after all."

"I'm glad you recognize that."

"Sure. Why, you're the bologna in our sandwich."

"Bologna?"

"No? The cheese in our panini?"

"Ew."

"The marshmallow. In our s'more of love."

She burst out laughing, and Marcus groaned, but smiled. Jace viewed them both with a mock frown. "I thought you liked food?"

"Ignore him. He was dropped on his head as a baby." Marcus pressed a chaste kiss against her forehead. "We take this day by day. I don't want you to feel rushed. It's not like we have to run out and get married." His lips quirked. "Though I'm sure Jace already has a venue picked out."

She glanced over her shoulder in time to see a dull flush cover Jace's high cheekbones, and he glared at his brother before switching a sheepish gaze to her face. "I've always liked Singer Island. But it's not like I've gone and booked a hotel or anything."

"Of course not." She twisted and kissed him full on the mouth before separating and looking at Marcus. "I think you should both go to counseling."

His eyebrows lowered and she held up her hand to forestall him. "It's important. For you and for me. Please, just think about it."

He stared at her hand stroking over his chest. "I'll think about it. For you."

"And like you said, we'll take it week by week."

"I actually said day by day."

"I'd say year by year, but I think it would scare you. I want you to stop worrying that one day I'll get bored and walk away from you. You're both stuck with me. My sisters are right in one aspect—when I love, I do it wholeheartedly. Don't make me regret it."

"You'll never regret it," Jace promised. "We waited too long for you. So, I say we take it month by month." He started to brush little kisses along her neck, making her abruptly aware of her near nakedness beneath her robe.

Marcus loosened the tie and kissed along her jaw to her

ear. When he reached there, she smiled to hear his whisper.

"Year by year."

# About the Author

Alisha Rai has been enthralled with romance novels since she smuggled her first tattered Harlequin home from the library at the age of thirteen. A mild-mannered florist by day, she pens sexy, emotional contemporaries and paranormals by night.

After a lifetime spent bouncing around the States, she is content to call sunny South Florida home for now. When she's not reading or working, Alisha loves to hang out with her close-knit family. She happily lives in a chaotic house filled with clutter, laughter, good food, boisterous kids and very loud relatives.

Alisha loves to hear from her readers! You can send her an e-mail at alishawrites@gmail.com or visit her on the web at www.alisharai.com.

*Sure, the sex is scorching hot, but can three hearts truly beat as one?*

# Our Man Friday

## *© 2008 Claire Thompson*

What's the old adage—sex ruins friendship? Cassidy lives it every day as she fights the lingering feelings for her ex, Ian. Still secretly, desperately in love with him, she settles for sharing a house and a business. Their lives are intertwined in every way...except the way she wants most.

Fear of commitment drove Ian to push his and Cassidy's romance back into his comfort zone—friendship. But things become decidedly uncomfortable when sexy Scotsman Kye McClellan enters the picture. As Cassidy's passion reignites, Ian is faced with the sudden prospect of losing the thing most precious to him.

Ian remains firmly in Cassidy's heart even as she succumbs to Kye's charms. Soon, as Kye's allure draws Ian in, she begins to wonder if she can have all she's ever wanted—plus one. Just as they all begin to tip into the white-hot cauldron of romance, Kye takes to his wanderlusting ways to avoid the burn. Ian and Cassidy are left with each other...and an even bigger missing piece than before.

All they can do is trust that love will somehow bring their gypsy-hearted lover home again.

*Warning: Explicit, erotic m/m/f passion. Double penetration takes on a whole new meaning—the hot and sensual combinations will leave you needing a cold shower!*

*Available now in ebook and print from Samhain Publishing.*

LaVergne, TN USA
27 December 2009

168124LV00004B/117/P